ANNA]

"Chock-full of secrets and spies, love and betrayal, danger and adventure, all of which is set against the devastating backdrop of WWI, Windswept by Annabelle McCormack is a sumptuous, fast-paced, and riveting read that'll have you cheering for the heroine until the very end."

— HANNAH MARY MCKINNON,
INTERNATIONALLY BESTSELLING AUTHOR

"Suspenseful, sexy, and moving, Windswept is a great choice for those looking for strong female leads in their historical fiction. Ginger will inspire you; the story will enthrall you; and the passionate romance will win you over."

— SAMANTHA HUI, INDEPENDENT BOOK
REVIEW

"Windswept is a delightful, ripsnorting adventure with a feisty heroine, a breathless pace, and endless adventure, intrigue, and romance. You will smile from cover to cover. This will remind you how enjoyable a good book can be."

— WILLIAM BERNHARDT, BESTSELLING
AUTHOR

A
ZEPHYR
RISING

ANNABELLE
MCCORMACK

Published by Annabelle McCormack

www.annabellemccormack.com

For all the feisty ladies, most especially my dear mother.

ALSO BY ANNABELLE MCCORMACK

Windswept: The Windswept Saga Book 1 (Order Here)

Sands of Sirocco: The Windswept Saga Book 2 (Available September 27, 2022: Preorder Now)

To find out the latest about my new releases, please sign up for my newsletter! I love hearing from readers and have some great offers lined up for my subscribers.

A ZEPHYR RISING

CHAPTER ONE

AUGUST 1914

SOMERSET, ENGLAND

$\mathcal{T}$he world had gone mad and Ginger Whitman couldn't stomach it for one more second.

She stood from her seat in the stone gazebo where she'd been attempting to read the newspaper. The paper crinkled in her gloved hand as she started across the lawn toward her family's home. One thing after another had distracted her: thoughts of guests arriving soon, the glare of the sun against the paper, the feeling of uselessness. The memory of the townspeople singing and chanting in the streets a few nights ago.

"It's a long way to Tipperary..."

She shuddered thinking of those excited faces and toasts. Since then, that tune had been stuck in her head, teasing and haunting her. According to the papers, the celebration had even extended to Buckingham Palace, where King George and Queen Mary greeted the merry crowds.

So many people cheering for the promise of death and destruction.

She slowed and bent toward the grass, righting a fallen croquet hoop. The servants had already set up games for the afternoon. Her palm grazed a mallet as she passed it.

She felt immune to the general sentiment pervading her country, unable to comprehend how something she'd always thought of as being so ugly and fearsome as *war* could now be called "splendid." She strolled under the shade of a tall elm and stopped, taking in her family's stately house. Servants bustled, setting up the garden party under the towering shade of the graceful arched windows overlooking the west balcony. Just this morning, all but one footman had given notice, explaining their intention to enlist. They walked now with a spring to their step, whistling, proud to do their bit.

Even this party felt incongruous to her. Parties were for peaceful times, for quiet moments while gazing over grassy hills. As though nature wanted to offer its agreement, a warm breeze wrapped her in a gentle embrace, but left goosebumps on her skin. The chill of autumn already crept into the fingertips of the wind.

She frowned and deposited her newspaper on a bench under the tree. The scent of ink remained on her gloves as she started forward again.

Anxiety had been clawing at her gut since the news had broken four days earlier. Britain was at war with Germany. The actions of six conspirators in Sarajevo in June had sealed the fates of many. The thought of men dying in combat on the battlefield made her throat clench. Which families would this war touch? Her friends? Or maybe her own brother?

Her mouth went dry.

The inexplicable buzz of excitement bothered her the most. The young men of her age who were eager to show their patriotism for king and country—none of them seemed to think beyond that. Even Henry seemed to share their lack of foresight. Her older brother had entered an impassioned discussion with a friend at dinner the previous night about volunteering before they were called up.

She didn't want life to change. Uncertainty about the future made the merriment around her feel like ignorance and naïveté. The declarations about "routing the Huns" in a few short weeks sounded like nothing more than hubris and bravado. Like many men she knew, Henry had only experienced shooting in hunts. Hunts ending with lawn parties and tea and baths. Servants to tend to their horses. She couldn't help but wonder if they would be so confident when another man was their target.

Worse still, she was completely powerless, silently screaming as she watched her life invaded by a force she had no ability to influence or help fight against. What if the war came to her doorstep?

The servants unfurled tablecloths, the white fabric catching like sails in the breeze, billowing and beautiful. Ginger steadied herself against the trunk of the tree, the fingertips of her gloves catching against the bark.

Weeks earlier, they'd been more concerned about the Americans winning the Henley Regatta. The familiar world of the London Season, with its late-night dinners, parades at Hyde Park, breathless balls, and thrilling cricket matches—it was slipping away. Eclipsed by something none of them quite understood. Only men like her father, who had served in the African war, carried on with gravitas.

For once in her life, her father's opinion seemed to be aligned with hers. She wished she could talk to him about it all. But he had barely spoken to her the last week. He continued to be angry with her.

Her jaw set. She didn't want to think about it. Or

Stephen's impending arrival. She wasn't ready to face him yet.

The open-aired tents that had been erected for the party swayed in the morning breeze and Ginger gave up her spot as she saw her mother among the servants. Mama had transformed their own garden party into a fundraising event to support the war effort.

This was a way to be useful. *For now.* She slipped under the cover offered by the tent where her mother stood. Both she and the head housekeeper, Mrs. Williams, wore deep frowns as they spoke.

A few days earlier, Ginger would have dismissed their concerns as something trivial. Given the new circumstances, it seemed worth asking about. Ginger paused at her mother's side. "What is it, Mama? Has something happened?"

Her mother's green-eyed gaze turned toward her. "The butcher's delivery never arrived from town this morning. And it's getting quite late. The kitchen is in chaos because the cook had several cold meat items on the menu."

Ginger imagined the scene. The party would start in five hours—'chaos' was likely too gentle a term. "Mr. Martin has always been punctual. What could have delayed him?"

Mrs. Williams cleared her throat, the soft lines by her eyes crinkling as her gaze swept over the tent. "That's what Lady Braddock and I are worried about. Someone might have done something to his business because..." She trailed off.

She didn't have to finish. Ginger understood the implication. Yesterday, the papers had carried tales of businesses being destroyed. While Ginger had dressed in the morning, her lady's maid had told her that over-zealous "patriots" had smashed the windows to the local bookseller's shop.

"You don't think someone might have harmed him because he's German?" Ginger straightened, alert with the horrifying thought. "But Mr. Martin is one of us—he's been in town longer than I've been alive. And his wife and children..."

Her mother put a gentle hand on her bare wrist. "We're sending Florence to go and check on the order. There isn't need for alarm yet."

The housemaid would be more useful at Penmore. And it would give her something to do instead of mill about and worry over the war and the looming confrontation with Stephen. Ginger shook her head. "I can go into town instead of Florence. I'd like to know if anything has happened sooner rather than later."

"You're a dear." Her mother's lips curved in an affectionate smile.

Ginger left the two older women in the tent and strode toward the house. Passing her lady's maid, Ginger turned. "Oh, Violet—I'll wear the striped dress I got in London two weeks ago. I'm going into town, so I won't have as much time to get ready for the party. If you don't mind—tend to Lucy first." Her younger sister would be happy to have Violet's attentions. She always complained about how long Ginger's hair took.

"Yes, my lady." Violet curtsied, her red hair gleaming in the sun. Henry joked Violet was well-suited to be Ginger's maid because only she understood the tribulations a redhead had in matching clothes to her hair. Ginger smiled to herself. The trait she shared with her maid *had* bonded them.

Only a week earlier, she and Violet had gushed over some of the latest styles coming in for the fall from Paris. She wouldn't use those types of dresses now. Then again, Henry seemed certain they would resolve the entire conflict by Christmas. Her father was more wary.

For weeks, Ginger had followed the building tensions between the governments of Europe in the papers. When the

Archduke of Austria and his wife had been shot in Bosnia, most Britons didn't believe it would lead to war with Germany. But Germany had been aggressive, hungry for war. Despite the many declarations of war between countries toward the end, she'd still hoped for peace. But when the Germans had refused to respect the neutrality of Belgium, the patience of the British government had ended.

Now it was all too late.

She found the chauffer in the courtyard, reading his newspaper. "I hope you made it further into the dreary news than I did," she said. "Would you give me a ride into town?"

Bosworth blinked at her from under his cap. "Right away, my lady." He frowned at his newspaper. "I expect they'll need good drivers in the army."

Not another one. She said nothing as he readied the motorcar. At the rate they were losing servants, she might have to learn to drive. Her lips twisted in amusement. That wouldn't be the worst thing.

The small village of Penmore was only a few minutes' drive from her family's estate. As the car wove its way over hills, Ginger reclined into the leather backseat of the car, a breeze blowing a few face-framing stray hairs into her eyes. The war had been declared the day after a bank holiday and so many people had been away. Her family had only just returned from London.

The familiar greys and whites of the stone buildings standing on either side of the main street of the hamlet set her heart at ease. The townspeople milled in the streets, on their way to the market. From the open market, the scents of freshly baked goods, cinnamon, and cooking food filled the air.

Home was the most welcome place to be right now. She only hoped all she loved about it would stay as it was.

The motorcar pulled up at the butcher shop and

Bosworth held the door for Ginger. She stepped out onto the street. A few women passed behind the car on foot, and continued around it, as though avoiding the pavement in front of the Martins' shop.

How odd.

Shutters hung over the front windows. Perhaps the Martins had heard what had happened to the bookseller's shop and wanted to protect their house? The front door appeared to be locked. She shook the knob in her hand and the door rattled with a hollow wooden sound—but didn't budge. The Martins lived behind the shop. Would they be there? Ginger gave an uneasy glance to Bosworth. "Wait here for me. I'm going to the back."

She unlatched the gate in the waist-high fence beside the house. The unpleasant, earthy scent of livestock mixed with chicken droppings stung her nose. She pulled out a perfumed handkerchief from her handbag and pressed it against her nostrils. A young goat stood on top of a small enclosure, its eyes fixed on her. Ginger adjusted her hat. A goat wouldn't attack her. But then again, what did she know about goats?

She edged her way toward the back of the house, staying close to the outer wall. The goat bleated, and she jumped. "I'm a friend," she whispered. The small horns on top of its head appeared more threatening than at first glance.

She turned the corner, and a sudden honk made her heartbeat thud. A large white goose flapped its wings at her. She pressed a hand over her racing heart and caught a breath. *Good gracious.* She was the one being a goose.

Hurrying the last few steps to the back door, Ginger paused. The animals continued to watch her curiously. If there was a war on the horizon, she needed to be made of stronger stuff than this. Twenty years of gentle breeding had done little to prepare her for anything. The skills she had learned in finishing school seemed awfully vapid, given what they might be facing.

She rapped on the door with the back of her knuckles. "Mr. Martin?"

From the window beside the door a pair of eyes peeked over the ledge. One of the Martin children, no doubt. Whispered voices followed, and then the child hid once more.

If something had happened, it was likely the Martin children were living in fear. Ginger tried again. "Mr. Martin. It's Virginia Whitman."

A few beats passed, and the lock scraped against the frame. The door opened a crack. Mrs. Martin stood there, her dark hair in disarray, her eyelids red and puffy. She wiped her hands on her apron. "Lady Virginia." Her voice was a hoarse whisper. "It's good of you to come." A girl no older than two clutched her skirt.

Something *was* wrong. Ginger tried to blanket her alarm, her reaction subdued. "Mrs. Martin, what's happened?"

Mrs. Martin took a furtive glance behind her and slipped out, pushing the toddler back inside. She closed the door. "How did you hear of it?" A glassy expression hazed her eyes —as though she hadn't slept.

A heavy feeling sank through Ginger. "I heard nothing, Mrs. Martin. We were waiting for Mr. Martin to arrive this morning with the order for the garden party. When he didn't turn up, I thought I would come and check on you."

Mrs. Martin covered her mouth with a crumpled handkerchief. "Oh, the garden party." Tears fell onto her cheeks. "I'm so sorry, my lady. They took Friedrich. My son John, too."

Ginger gasped. "Taken? By whom?"

Mrs. Martin dabbed at her eyes. "Officials came to the house with papers, arrested them." She sobbed. "They've imprisoned them both."

"Imprisoned?" Friedrich Martin was one of the kindest men in town. What had he done to deserve imprisonment? "Surely they've made a mistake."

"There's no mistake." Mrs. Martin sniffled. "It's because of the Aliens Restriction Act. He's German. And now I'm terrified they're coming for the rest of us. The police have ordered me to report to them every day." The words brought a fresh round of tears.

Report to them? Whatever for? Ginger gathered the distraught woman into her arms. "But Mrs. Martin—you're an Englishwoman. You have nothing to fear."

Mrs. Martin shook her head. "I lost my citizenship when I married Friedrich. Women must adopt their husband's, you see. I'm so very frightened for my children." She gulped and pulled away from Ginger. "I'm sorry, Lady Virginia. I shouldn't carry on like this in front of you. You're practically a child yourself."

Ginger stiffened. The statement made her feel as though Mrs. Martin thought of Ginger as naïve and overprotected.

She took a steadying breath. Mrs. Martin couldn't have meant it as an insult. After all, Ginger only debuted a couple of years earlier, and the townsfolk still referred to her and her younger sister Lucy as the "Whitman girls."

"You've had a terrible shock. I'm honored you've trusted me." Ginger furrowed her brow. "I hope it isn't horribly insensitive for me to ask—but what reason did they give for arresting John? He was born here."

Regret filled Mrs. Martin's expression. "Unfortunately not. Friedrich thought it would be useful if his mother helped me with John, as he was my first-born and my mother died when I was a girl. He was born in Germany and spent the first three months of his life there."

A thump behind the door reminded Ginger of the children inside. "Mrs. Martin, what can we do? How can I help you? Surely my father will assist you." In times like these, her father's earldom—as well as his work in the Foreign Office—might be more influential to people like the Martins.

"I'd be so grateful for you to make some inquiries about Friedrich and John's whereabouts." She gripped Ginger's forearm tightly. "What if they've sent them to Germany?"

The thought was frightening. Ginger knew little about the Aliens Restriction Act, but surely they had more decency than to repatriate honest men with homes and families in England?

"I'm certain my father will help get Mr. Martin and John back home, if he can." Ginger put a hand on Mrs. Martin's shoulder. "In the meantime, do you and your children have all you need?" How was the woman to feed and care for seven children without her husband?

Mrs. Martin wrung her hands, her handkerchief fluttering to the ground. Her face reddened. "For now. I don't have the money for the order until Friedrich returns, Lady Virginia. I apologize, we can't fill the order. The farmer never brought our own order yesterday."

Ginger regretted having mentioned the order at all. "Oh, never mind that. We'll make do." Ginger dropped her hand to her side. "But if you need anything at all, Mrs. Martin, please let me know. We all must care for each other, especially during these precarious times."

The statement sounded hollow to Ginger as she rode back toward Penmore, replaying the conversation in her mind. She should have offered to cancel the debt entirely, even if it wasn't her place to do so. Or offered them food and shelter.

She would talk to her mother. They'd return tomorrow with some money. Her mother wouldn't let the Martins go hungry. And Ginger was sure the church would have resources to help them.

But why had the police arrested John, too? He was a boy, just sixteen.

The chauffeur swung the car around a pothole and the entire frame jolted in response, bumping her against the side. Dust flew up and Ginger waved it away, distractedly.

Something had to be done for the Martins.

CHAPTER TWO

Ginger hastened into the library, removing her hat as she approached her father. He stood by one of the tall windows in the room, *glancing through a long, official-looking letter.*

She slowed as she drew closer to him. Her father's gaze was pensive, focused outside. His face was half in shadow. The silver streaks in his dark hair stood out in the dim light. She caught her breath, feeling like she had as a young girl. Back then, she'd always had orders not to disturb her father.

Obeying the order had been tricky, considering how much she'd loved the library. Even now, the scent of it—old books and sweet pipe tobacco—made her want to curl up in a nook and read.

A floorboard creaked under her feet and her father looked up. His brow furrowed as he studied her expression. "You look flushed. Should I ring for the doctor?"

He must have been truly concerned. Her father was rarely an alarmist.

"No, I'm well, thank you." Ginger fidgeted with her hat. "Father—I've just come from town." She sat on a sofa by the fireplace. "Mr. Martin never came with the order for the kitchen this morning. He couldn't because the police have arrested him. John Martin, too. Mrs. Martin mentioned something about the Aliens Restriction Act."

Her father lifted his thick, dark eyebrows. "John?" He didn't seem surprised about Mr. Martin, though.

"Apparently, he was born in Germany. We must help them." Ginger placed her hands on her lap, though her fingers curled in. Her father had already appeared to be troubled when she'd arrived. Perhaps she'd caught him in a foul mood. Either way, behaving emotionally would make her plea seem immature.

"And they never thought to naturalize?" Her father grimaced. "I'm uncertain much can be done. Foreign nationals of military age will all be under intense scrutiny. And in some ways, it may be for their own safety. There have been attacks on the German-born in England already."

She bit her lip. She hadn't thought of that.

Not having even considered the opposite perspective made her feel foolish.

Still, the anguish on Mrs. Martin's face at being separated from her husband and son reminded her it wasn't so simple. And John Martin couldn't help his parents' decision not to naturalize. "But John is as English as I am, raised here. His mother was born here. And all his siblings are British subjects."

Her father tapped the letter in his hands against the window frame. "There may be a better case for the younger Martin than the old codger. He was a fool not to have the young man naturalized years ago—or do so himself. But everything is changing quickly now." He was silent for a few beats, then drew in a sharp breath, straightening. "I'll make some inquiries with a solicitor. See what can be done."

At least his practical side didn't prevent his willingness to help. Relieved, Ginger relaxed her shoulders. "Mrs. Martin asked if you could learn their whereabouts. The poor woman is terrified the government may repatriate them back to Germany."

"And with good reason. Not everyone will have as much sympathy for the Martins as you and I. But consider the fact that repatriation might be better than being imprisoned for however long this war lasts."

The hypocrisy of it infuriated Ginger. She huffed. "The king himself has German relatives—including the Kaiser."

"Yes, and see how well that familial relationship worked out for the whole of Europe. It's why we're in this mess." Her father's gaze followed the swirl of dust motes swimming in the sunlight pouring through the windows. With a look of resignation in his face, he moved toward a secretary against the wall. "Mrs. Martin would do well to stay indoors for a few weeks."

Ginger stood. She'd thought her father would show more alarm over the matter than he had. "And that's it then? You'll inquire with a solicitor, and she should stay indoors?"

"Dear girl, what more would you have me do? I have many far more pressing matters." Her father opened a drawer and put away the letter he'd held. "The Foreign Office is already calling me to a new post."

No wonder. Ginger cringed. The news would devastate her mother. "For the army?" She hadn't thought her father would be amongst the first to be asked to serve.

"To service in their offices in Cairo." A tired expression crossed her father's face, a muscle twitching in his jaw. "They want me ready to board a ship in a fortnight."

Cairo? Ginger's jaw slackened. The whole family had spent a year in Cairo when she was seven—she still remembered some of the Arabic her Egyptian governess had taught her. Warm memories of sitting on open verandahs, stealing sips of sweet tea spiced with cardamom, and skipping by busy markets came rushing back. "But..." Ginger blinked rapidly, taking his words in. "Why Cairo?"

"There's concern about the allegiances of the Ottomans. If they enter the war with an alliance to Germany, there will be a need to transition the khedivate into something more friendly to the British. The Suez Canal could be at risk."

Her father spoke of that area of the world with an ease which displayed his expertise. She made a mental note to borrow some of his books on Egypt and Arabia from the library later—brush up on her own understanding of the Arab world.

Then another, more worrisome thought occurred to her. "Wait—a fortnight? Just you? Or will you be taking us all to Cairo?" Wartime life here at Penmore had seemed daunting enough. But if they all went to Cairo...

The changes to their lives would be drastic. Far more than she'd considered. She toyed with her necklace apprehensively.

"We still have the house in Cairo, which is more than adequate and comfortable accommodation for the family. Really, it will come down to the wishes of your mother." Her father rubbed his jaw and gave her a stern look. "No one is to know of this, though."

"Of course." Despite her father's sober demeanor, she appreciated when he gave her a straight answer, rather than telling her it was of no concern to her. She eyed the secretary where he'd placed the letter. She suspected he'd just learned of the assignment himself, given his behavior. Was he afraid? Disturbed? He certainly didn't seem to welcome the news. "Have you told mother yet?"

What would her mother say about going to Cairo? Mama wouldn't be happy to have the family separated.

"Not yet. I don't want to put anything else on her this

afternoon. She's thrown herself into transforming this garden party into a fundraiser so admirably. No need to upset her now."

Ginger nodded. Given how unsettling the news about the Martins was, it would be more than enough to worry her mother for now. "That reminds me—I should go and warn her there won't be a butcher order. Thank you for promising to investigate the matter for the Martins." She headed toward the door.

"The Fishers will attend this afternoon, won't they? I believe I heard from your mother they're invited."

Ginger froze mid-step. Her back grew taut as she swiveled her head over her shoulder. "Yes." She'd hoped to avoid this conversation before the party.

"And?" Her father folded his hands in front of him.

A burning sensation rose in her esophagus. If she'd experienced any joy at the declaration of war, it had been as it regarded to this: she'd hoped the war would allow her to delay answering Stephen altogether. An engagement seemed an odd thing to consider while everyone else concerned themselves with looming battlefronts. "And I still haven't changed my mind."

"Stephen deserves your answer, Virginia. And we could still just about arrange a wedding before this conflict takes him away." Her father's lip curled under his trim moustache. Her chest tightened. She hated when he put so much pressure on her.

"In just two weeks? I hardly think so. Besides which, I gave him my answer." Prickles went up the back of her neck. "The only reason I even agreed to consider the matter further is because you demanded I must. In which case, I need more time." Ginger thought of the giant diamond Stephen had flashed when he'd proposed two weeks before. A beautiful jewel straight from his family's diamond mines in

Kimberley. "I told him I'd give him my definitive answer in a month and I intend to."

She wished she'd had the strength to refuse to reconsider. She already knew what her answer would be—didn't she? The thought of marriage to Stephen made her ill.

"He was practically a fixture at your side all Season." Her father's dark brown eyes glittered. "And you've always known my wishes for you both."

Those wishes had led to this current unpleasantness. She was too fond of her father to argue with him again—doing so after Stephen's proposal had kept her up many nights the last few weeks. Their relationship had never been less than cordial. Her father expressed his admiration for her in ways that made her feel respected. She didn't want to disappoint his expectations.

"He was by my side because Henry was around—not because I welcomed his company." Ginger gritted her teeth. She hadn't been able to get rid of Stephen, in fact.

Her father bristled, obviously as irritated as she. "You can't put him off, Virginia. What reason can you possibly have for refusing him?"

"To begin with, I don't particularly trust him, Father. Or like him much." Ginger dipped her chin defensively. She wouldn't mention the way he acted so possessively of her. "It may be easy enough for you to marry me off to him. But there are many other wealthy, respectable gentlemen out there, if you're worried."

"You may accuse me of being unromantic, but Stephen has loved you for years. You haven't given him the chance he deserves." Her father sighed. "Not to mention the match is something our families both wish for."

Much as she hated to be the only one opposed to the apparent happiness for everyone, Ginger set her lips in a firm line. Arguing with her father was pointless. He would accuse her of being too young to know what she wanted, as he'd done before.

"Papa—" she rarely used the term, but now seemed a good time "—you must trust me to decide about this. I have to be married for life to whomever I choose, after all. What if I want more than Stephen is offering? You can hardly fault me for hoping to love the man I marry." More than that, she longed for the thrill of romance, even if she wouldn't admit it to her father.

Her father approached, his posture as perfect as ever. He held out a hand for her and she offered one. Gently, he patted her hand between his. "Hard days lie in store for us all, Virginia. I'd like to see you settled with a young man who can provide for you and give you all the comfort you need. Stephen's a wealthy man already. You'll want for nothing with him. And in time, you may even grow to love him. If it's the fact that he's not the heir to Lord Knotley's title—"

If love made one's skin crawl the way Stephen's attentions did hers, she wanted nothing to do with him. "It's the man, not the title. Though, to be honest, I find Rufus Fisher a much nicer prospect. Think he'll divorce his wife for me?" She smiled jauntily.

Her father's eyes widened, aghast.

Ginger chuckled, and she leaned forward and kissed his cheek. "Don't worry, I'd never bring scandal to the family. Besides which, I'm not interested in Rufus, either."

"I know you wouldn't." He squeezed her hand warmly.

Ginger turned back and hurried out of the library before her father said anything more. Ginger heard him chuckle softly as she closed the library door behind her. Beyond the hall, Henry descended the massive staircase gracing the heart of the stately house, newspaper in one hand.

Henry would want to know about the Martins. "Going somewhere?" She fell into step beside him.

"Not precisely." Henry eyed her. "Shouldn't you be getting ready for the garden party?"

"Not quite yet." Ginger spotted Mrs. Williams crossing the foyer. "Oh—Mrs. Williams, would you be so kind as to tell mother there won't be any delivery from Mr. Martin today, after all? I'll be outside to explain it to you both directly."

"I'll tell her ladyship immediately." Mrs. Williams' face was sober as she rushed out of the foyer.

"No delivery for the garden party? What is the world coming to?" Henry grinned and ran a hand through the dark locks of hair over his forehead. "Now, what is it you needed?"

Ginger motioned for him to follow her. "The delivery leads to a much bigger issue and partially why I wanted to see you." Ginger paused as Henry opened the door to the parlor for them. They went into the room and Ginger recounted the way she'd found Mrs. Martin earlier.

Henry slapped his newspaper on a table beside a settee. "That's outrageous. John Martin is no threat. And neither is his father. And how is the woman supposed to scrape by in their absence?"

Thank goodness. Henry had often been her refuge in disagreements with her father. "My point exactly. Father seems preoccupied, though. Is there anything you and I can do about it?"

Henry frowned. "What did father say?"

"He said he'd ask a solicitor." Much as Henry often spoke boldly, he rarely went too far outside their father's wishes. Would he defer to her father here, also?

Henry drummed his fingers on the table. "I'll see who I can get to help. A solicitor may help see about naturalization, but I don't know if that'll be enough. We may need to speak to someone within the Home Secretary's office." He gave Ginger a serious look. "But you should prepare yourself for there being little we can do. They passed the Aliens Restriction Act for good reason. Now that we're at war, Germany won't hesitate to reach her fingers into the country with spies. And there are many likely already here, waiting for instructions."

His words made worry snake its way tightly around her chest, strangulating her. Could there really be spies among them? Even in places like Penmore? *No.* They were safe here.

But they may not even be staying here. Did Henry know about Cairo? She wanted to discuss the matter with *someone.* If they went to Cairo, who knew how long they would be there?

The door opened and the butler, Mr. Pierce, stepped inside. He came toward them. "Lord Stephen Fisher is here to see you, my lord."

The worry about spies seemed to dwindle compared to seeing Stephen right now. She wasn't ready to talk to him. Ginger's eyes darted to the door, hoping she had time to escape.

A tall, thin man, Mr. Pierce had a keen eye—and always seemed to guess the gravity of the situation at hand. "Would you prefer for me to wait to let him in until you've slipped away?" Mr. Pierce asked Ginger.

"Pierce, don't indulge her." Henry's words were dry. His loyalty to Stephen had always been at the expense of what Ginger wanted.

Ginger ground her teeth. She gave Mr. Pierce a grateful look. "Yes, please." She headed toward the back exit.

"You won't be able to avoid Stephen at the party," Henry called behind her. He crossed his arms.

"Don't remind me." Ginger cut her eyes at him, but smiled. "But I can avoid him now." Henry knew what she thought of his best friend and fortunately never tried to press the issue beyond a gentle ribbing.

She would have appreciated him telling Stephen to let the matter rest, though. Instead, he only seemed to tell Ginger to adjust herself to the idea.

She raced from the room into a darkened hallway leading to a back staircase. Her life felt as though it was being placed in a vise—everything more uncertain than ever. This was going to be a long party indeed.

CHAPTER THREE

The music from the string quartet drifted through the trees and Ginger fingered her champagne flute with gloved hands. Guests strolled over the lawn, enjoying the perfect weather. Small groups formed clusters throughout the grass—the groundskeeper would grumble to see all the pits from the women's heels come morning.

When she'd been younger, Ginger had watched the women in their beautiful dresses from the windows of the house, wishing to join them on the lawn. The garden parties then had seemed like a wonderful adventure—romantic, too. A chance to smile at a handsome young man, to feel the thrill of love.

Her own experiences had been quite different.

"It won't be long before parties like this are but a memory," a familiar woman's voice said behind her, breaking into her thoughts.

Ginger's mouth opened. Her friend, Charlotte Thompson, stood there, a picture of grace. A lace parasol rested against her shoulder. The last big event Ginger had attended before coming home from London had been Charlotte and

Robert's wedding. "What are you doing here?" Ginger hugged her. "You're supposed to be on your honeymoon."

"Yes, well," Charlotte pushed a perfect dark curl behind her ear, "Robert decided it was too dangerous for us to continue abroad. And we were having the most wonderful tour of France."

They weren't the only ones caught by terrible timing for their trips. A few ladies Ginger had talked to this afternoon had mentioned their ruined holidays. Ginger gripped her arm. "And where is your groom?"

Charlotte shrugged and toyed with the single strand of pearls around her neck. "Heaven knows. Probably chumming it with your brother. If he can lure Henry away from Angelica Fisher. Henry looks absolutely besotted with her, by the way."

Did it bother Charlotte to see Henry moving on? Ginger couldn't tell from Charlotte's expression. But, then again, she'd chosen Robert over Henry. And she'd been a radiant bride. "Henry is easily besotted." Ginger sipped her champagne. "I can't tell you how relieved I am you're here. I've been hiding from Henry and his friends and it's been quite lonely."

"You mean you've been hiding from Stephen." Charlotte smirked. "Aren't you hoping for a double wedding? You with Stephen. Henry with Angelica." She guffawed softly. "The whole thing seems incestuous."

Ginger's cheeks warmed. Only Charlotte seemed to understand her dislike of Stephen. "Oh, Charlotte—what on earth am I to do? The man refuses to leave me alone."

A footman paused in front of them with cucumber sandwiches on a silver platter. They declined. "You could tell him no." Charlotte adjusted her parasol. "You don't want to marry him."

If only it were so easy. Then again, Charlotte had been

away when Stephen had proposed. She didn't know what
had happened when she'd told Stephen no. "I did. But my
father has made his expectations clear. Forced me to tell him
I needed a month to consider his proposal. And it's not as
though I have other offers coming my way."

Marriage was her destiny. The only adventure to liven up
her routine-choked life. Or so she'd been told. And if they
didn't settle her situation soon, people would call her an old
maid.

Another footman came by with champagne, which Charlotte accepted. She twirled the stem in her fingertips and the
light bouncing through it threw reflections on the grass.
"Because Stephen has frightened all other potential suitors
away."

Irritation pricked her throat. Charlotte wasn't exaggerating. All the young men in her circle assumed she was
Stephen's intended, both from his possessiveness and his
attentiveness. Given his status and wealth, few would dare to
cross him. "If those potential suitors aren't willing to stand
up to Stephen, I'm uncertain they'd interest me."

Charlotte frowned. "What you need to do is make a secret
attachment elsewhere. Outside all the usual circles of our
friends." She scanned the lawn. "Now who can we fix you up
with?"

A secret attachment? Ginger couldn't think of anything
more unlikely.

"Ginny, Henry was asking for you—" Lucy came scram-
bling up. Her stylish hat sat smartly over her braided dark
brown hair. She stopped by Charlotte. "Oh, I'm sorry to
interrupt."

"It's fine." Ginger smiled at her sister. She remembered
being fourteen years old at garden parties. Old enough to feel
she should be part of the conversation, young enough to feel

she still belonged in the nursery. "Lucy, you remember my friend Charlotte?"

"How do you do?" Lucy curtsied. She inspected Charlotte's elegant attire briefly before turning her gaze to Ginger. "Henry said it was important."

Ginger exchanged a glance with Charlotte, an uneasy feeling coming over her. "I suppose if it's important."

Charlotte smiled at Ginger encouragingly. "I'll go with you."

Lucy adjusted her hat. "What do you think of my frock? Will Angelica like it? Is it as fancy as hers? She won't mind me bothering her. I haven't seen her all summer and I'm eager to hear all about her debut ball."

Ginger remembered when the girls she'd gone to finishing school with had debuted before her, she'd felt a similar hesitation in knowing if their friendship would survive their new status as an adult.

Ginger had never paid too much attention to Angelica, as she'd always considered her one of Lucy's friends. After Angelica's debut this year and Henry's sudden attachment to her, she'd become part of Ginger's circle, rather than Lucy's. Not that Ginger found much to say to the quiet Fisher girl. What she lacked in personality, she more than made up for in looks, though, and her debut had been a smashing success.

"I'm sure Angelica would be glad to see you, Lucy. She'll likely welcome the break from Henry and his cabal," Ginger said. The three women crossed the lawn toward a tent, Lucy leading the way.

As they drew closer, Ginger caught sight of Stephen Fisher, who simpered at Henry's side. Henry and Stephen's friendship went back to infancy. If she refused Stephen, she didn't want to be the source of a rift between the two. Given that Stephen had made his intentions with Ginger known, her refusal would wound his pride in a manner he would consider publicly humiliating.

Stephen wore a hat over his straw-colored hair, the flat brim shading his eyes. Ginger couldn't tell if he'd seen her yet. *Into the lion's den.* She restrained the urge to hold her breath. If only Stephen wasn't well-liked, it would be so much easier to explain to everyone. Yet he was charming and affable, respected, and handsome.

Maybe she was being foolish.

But where her family seemed to find his attentions to her romantic, the way he looked at and touched her repulsed her. She shivered and pushed her feelings deep down.

"Ah, there's my darling sister." Henry stood from his seat at a round table, where some of his friends were gathered. He grinned at Ginger and then gave a quick wink to Lucy. "And you, too, Lucy."

Lucy's cheeks reddened. But she wouldn't dare retort in front of their guests.

Angelica sat beside Henry. "Angelica. My mother was inquiring about you. Lucy can take you to her," Ginger said. Hopefully, Lucy would have the time she sought with her friend.

Lucy gave Ginger a grateful look as Angelica stood. The willowy blonde held out an arm for Lucy and they left, whispering together. Ginger slid into the seat Angelica had vacated, still avoiding Stephen's gaze. She practically felt the weight of his stare. Charlotte rejoined her husband's side after greeting Henry.

Much as it had stung Henry when Charlotte had chosen Robert over him, Charlotte was right—Henry didn't seem nearly as bothered about it now that Angelica had become the object of his affections. "I'm glad you hurried over." Henry lifted a teacup to his lips. "I was telling the fellows of the Martins and it so happens Stephen may know someone who can help."

Ginger cringed inwardly. She wished Henry wouldn't have said anything to his friends. Especially not Stephen. Stephen sat across from her and her face flushed. "How wonderful." She smiled at Stephen. "I'd be so grateful for your help. Poor Mrs. Martin is devastated."

Stephen reclined back in his chair. "Of course, you realize the Aliens Restriction Act passed unanimously. You aren't likely to find too many sympathetic to the Germans now."

The weight of additional eyes and ears weighed on their conversation. Ginger wished her champagne glass wasn't empty—it made it so much easier to act calm when she had some object in which to direct her nervous energy. How like Stephen to insert his authoritative, smug attitude into everything. "I'm not sympathetic to the Germans. Only the Martins. Mr. Martin has been here for years. His wife is English. It seems to me a travesty to arrest him and his son for the crime of having been born in another country."

"A country with which we are currently at war," Stephen countered. A few of Henry's friends nodded and murmured in agreement. "The papers have been warning of spies in our midst for the last couple of years."

"But Mr. Martin isn't a spy." Ginger's anger grew. She pleaded to Henry with a look. He could silence Stephen's attempts to embarrass her this way.

"How do you know?" Stephen shrugged. "I'd venture to say there are many who are sympathetic to the Germans, right under your nose. What does a German spy look like? They aren't very good ones if they wear their allegiance like a button on their lapel."

Henry set his teacup on its saucer. "Ginny's right to be concerned about the Martins, though. We can't rightfully assume anyone with German ancestry must be sympathetic to their cause, can we, Fisher?"

Something in Henry's words chastened Stephen. He cleared his throat and his smile to Ginger faltered. "I was merely playing devil's advocate. It's good for Ginny to know what she's up against."

Under the tent, the clink of silverware against porcelain interrupted the din of conversation occasionally. Guests sat at their tables listening to the strains of the violins while footmen served ices.

She met Charlotte's encouraging gaze briefly. "I know what I'm up against, Stephen. I'm up against a group of individuals who would rather not bother with the trials that are changing the lives of a few people who they consider beneath them."

Ginger stood. "If you're able to help, as Henry suggested in the first place, I'd be grateful for it. Otherwise, I don't need the education you seem so eager to provide."

She sped away from the tent, furious for allowing Stephen to rankle her in front of their friends. Henry would be upset with her for acting impulsively. A breeze caught her hat. She held on to the brim, her face flaming. Why couldn't she control herself? She'd done so well over the Season, being polite and smiling. Laughing at jokes and even enjoying vapid conversations of no actual substance. But Stephen's proposal meant she could no longer pretend it wasn't all heading into something more.

The sounds of the party faded as she headed into the immaculately landscaped hedges forming a wall around one garden. She pushed a gate to the side and slipped inside, longing for privacy.

"Ginny!" Stephen caught her by the elbow as she moved to close the gate.

Ugh. Why did he always have to follow her? She gritted

her teeth. "I don't appreciate being made fun of. I care about this. What happens to the Martins is about so much more than them. How can we turn a blind eye to the good people caught in this situation?"

He encroached on her space. Slipping both hands onto her shoulders, his fingertips curled over her collarbone. Too close and intimate. She stiffened. "I didn't intend to poke fun at you, but I apologize. I love you, Ginny. I had hoped you would give me your answer by now." His thumbs rubbed gentle circles over the tense knots on her shoulders, making goosebumps rise on her neck.

She pulled away and turned, leveling her gaze at him. "I'm not sure I'm ready to be married."

A frustrated look crossed Stephen's face, and he stepped back. "Not ready? Ginny, we're about to go to war. Who knows what it will mean for me in the coming months? Either you'll marry me or you won't. It's simple. We're compatible in every way. And I'd give you all the privilege and prestige worthy of your name. You'd want for nothing with me."

The hum of bees amidst the sweet perfume of flowers ought to have been more comforting than it was right now.

"But it's not simple. I—" She caught her breath, trying to find the right words. He took her hand, his skin feeling cool against hers. His unwelcome touch made her stomach quiver. Staring at his hand, she clenched her jaw. "I want to know it's the right choice for my life. For both of us."

He laughed and reached into his breast pocket for a cigarette case. "You know it is. Both our families have always known. There isn't any doubt in my mind we should be together. I'm astounded you seem to think there is."

"But this has nothing to do with the Martins. You should help me regardless of whether I agree to marry you. You should help me because it's the decent thing to do."

Stephen lit a cigarette and stepped closer to her. "I only want to protect you, Ginny. If you'd let me, I'd have married you years ago. I'll always dream of you." His hand slipped behind her back, drawing her in more closely.

He'd ignored her. Burning with latent fury, Ginger craned her neck away from the scent of tobacco smoke. "Did you tell Henry you'd help me in order to corner me like this or because you can actually help?"

Stephen blew a stream of smoke from the corner of his lips. His eyes narrowed. "Cornered?" He took another drag from his cigarette. "Perhaps you should think more carefully about how you're speaking to me. If I could help, you wouldn't be so rude, would you?"

She looked him directly in the eye. "Can you help me or not?"

"I can help you." Stephen ran his fingers over the edge of her collarbone, then traced the back of his knuckle against her jawline. "It so happens a friend of mine works for the Home Secretary. I can send him an urgent message. Let him know about this situation and see what he can do." Stephen's look was stern. "But I can't make any promises, Ginny. It will take more than your word alone to assure them the younger Martin isn't a spy."

Ginger longed to step away from him but couldn't. Not when he held the cards. "What about Mr. Martin?"

"I doubt we can do much for him. His refusal to nationalize won't speak in his favor. But I'll ask." His eyes scanned hers as though gauging her response to his touch.

"Thank you." The idea of Stephen acting as her intermediary didn't entirely comfort her. "What's your friend's name at the Home Secretary's office? So I know who to tell my father to send a note to?"

Stephen's gaze strayed, as though to make sure they were alone. Would he attempt something like a kiss, knowing he had the means to manipulate her? She held her breath. A bird's wings fluttered as it landed in a fountain further in the garden. The bird titled its head, watching her with a beady dark eye. If only she had wings to fly away, like it did.

After a moment, he said, "David Peterson. But tell him to wait until I've made inquiries." He held out his hand. "Now. Since that's behind us, care to stroll back to the tent as friends? We wouldn't want everyone to believe we've been having any sort of unpleasantness."

Behave. She resisted the urge to flee. She'd feel less trapped with both feet in a peat bog than she did with him.

She smiled, relieved, and took his hand. "I can't tell you how grateful I am for your help."

As they made their way toward the tent, Ginger searched for Charlotte. She spotted her standing beside her husband, smiling. Robert was in animated conversation with her about something.

Her heart lurched. Charlotte could have married the future Earl of Braddock. She'd rejected Henry for Robert—a man whose family name did not appear in *Burke's Peerage*.

She wished she could simply tell him no, be done with it. Defy her father and not worry about the consequences. But was she as brave as Charlotte?

CHAPTER FOUR

*S*itting down to breakfast the next morning, Ginger nodded at her father and Henry. They paused from their quiet, serious discussion with wordless greetings. Her father had the newspaper open. "Not more bad news?" Ginger asked. She wished she could breakfast in bed like her mother did and avoid morning discussions. Not that she minded the politics—she didn't like mornings.

But breakfast in bed was a privilege extended only to married women. Unfortunately.

"It's all bad news when we're at war." Lucy made a face. "I still don't see why any Englishman should have to go and fight a battle over what's happening in Serbia."

"Nor should you have to worry." Henry pulled at a curl from Lucy's dark ponytail. "You should be able to enjoy playing with dolls and riding ponies."

"I'm fourteen, not four." Lucy straightened her shoulders and lifted her chin. Ginger suppressed a laugh. Lucy's awkward attempts to seem grown had increased lately. Maybe because of her own uncertainty about the future.

Lucy gave her father a sharp look. "You don't think the war will mean any delay in my going to Brillantmont, do you?"

"It may. Swiss finishing schools are hardly a priority, and we all have to make sacrifices." With a somber expression, he sighed and added, "You may as well know, as I've already told the rest of the family. I'm being called to serve in Cairo at the Foreign Office."

"Cairo?" Lucy's lips formed a round "o" with the last syllable. "That dreadful place? All I remember is flies and heat. When do you have to go?"

It surprised Ginger that she remembered anything from Cairo at all. Ginger barely did. More than likely, Lucy's "memories" were little more than stories they'd recounted over the years.

Her father lifted his teacup and spoke over the rim. "You mean when do 'we' go?"

What?

Lucy gasped, upsetting her glass of water. As the footman rushed to mop it up, Ginger leaned back, trying to keep her own reaction muted. Her mother must have insisted they all go. Would her father be expecting them all to leave in two weeks?

Despite so many unknowns, the idea of seeing something as iconic as the pyramids made her smile.

The lack of surprise on her brother's face, though, told her he already knew more about this than she did. "Is the family going?" Ginger asked.

Her father nodded. "Well, you may not. Depending on your decision with Stephen. But I'm afraid the rest of us will be. Maintaining two households during the war will be expensive. And your mother would prefer for us to stay together, given the distance. I'll be recommending Henry for a post with me."

Lucy's face had blanched. "You mean I have to go to

Egypt?" Her fingers trembled as she fussed with the serviette on her lap. "Can't I stay here at Penmore? Until I go to Brillantmont?"

Her father hadn't said it outright yet, but Ginger couldn't help thinking there wouldn't be a Brillantmont in Lucy's near future. *Poor Lucy.* Her devastation would be complete.

"We'll be closing the house, leaving it to operate on a reduced staff. There won't be anyone to care for you here, Lucy, nor would your mother want you left behind." Her father's look was sympathetic. "I know it isn't what you want, and I'm sorry. But, in time, the war will end and we can come back. With any luck, we'll be back by the beginning of next year."

Lucy appeared crestfallen. "An entire half a year? I don't want to spend a half a year in Egypt!" Tears formed in her eyes, and she shot an angry look toward Ginger. "Why does she get to stay?"

Ginger winced. She understood Lucy's disappointment, even if it wasn't one she shared completely. Their lives were in upheaval. Lucy couldn't understand that by giving Ginger the option to stay, all her father was really doing was putting more pressure on her to marry Stephen. Heat crawled up Ginger's neck.

"Virginia may go with us—but if she marries Stephen, then she'll have to stay here with her husband. She's a grown woman, therefore her options include staying and starting a household of her own. Then she can avoid Cairo altogether."

Did her father think she wasn't willing to go? She'd endure Egypt if it meant getting away from Stephen. The idea had enormous appeal.

"But didn't you say you're expected to board a ship in a fortnight?" Ginger played with her necklace. Was the entire house to shut by then?

"A fortnight?" Lucy's voice was close to a shriek.

Her father's brows furrowed sternly. "Yes, that's right."

Surely her father didn't expect her to get married to Stephen in two weeks if she stayed? "That's an awfully rushed engagement if I were to accept Stephen."

The scent of warm toast and butter filled the air as one footman served breakfast. Her father appeared thoughtful for a few moments. "I don't know if we can help the compressed timeline. Your mother might be keen on staying a few extra weeks to plan and hold a wedding, but I wouldn't be able to be a part of it."

"Or I could simply wait to marry until after the war." Ginger smiled tautly and met her father's gaze. "And go with you to Egypt. I'd love to go back there and see it all with fresh eyes. Brush up on my Arabic."

Her father quirked one brow, as though surprised at her lack of distress.

"You always paid more attention to your lessons than I did." Silverware clinked as Henry lifted his fork. "Finding antiquities was too distracting. I'll enjoy seeing those old pyramids and souks once again. Can't say I ever felt quite so adventurous as when I was there."

"That's because you were allowed to go exploring." Some of the old jealousy Ginger had felt as a girl came back as she lifted her fork.

The newspaper rustled as her father folded it. "Pout if you like, Virginia, but the Egyptian sun was very rough on your fair skin—you may not remember the sunburns you wailed about. You'd have to face those now, I'd imagine."

Ginger's lips twitched as she stifled a laugh. Her poor father was clearly irritated she was more than willing to go to Egypt.

"I don't want to go at all." Lucy waved her glass of juice. "And I don't see it's fair the only one who gets a choice is Ginny."

Ginger reached for a teacup. "I'm still not completely satisfied by my options, either. Much as I'd like to go to Egypt, leaving in two weeks seems extreme. And what of the Martins, Father? Will there be time to tend to this situation with them before you go? And if we aren't successful—I had thought to offer them refuge here at Penmore, if it came to it."

Henry made a choking noise, then patted his fist over his chest. He looked at Ginger as though she'd gone mad. Her father's expression was unreadable.

Lucy scraped butter over her toast. "Who are the Martins?"

"The butcher and his family." Henry gave Ginger an odd look. "Did you mention the idea to Mother yet?"

"The butcher?" Lucy's eyes widened. "As in the foul-smelling old man from the village?" Her knife remained frozen in mid-air by her toast. "Why on earth would you have them stay here?"

Lucy's snobbery was unsurprising. But it disappointed Ginger. The lack of charity and sensitivity might be second nature for a child, but Lucy was getting to an age where those tendencies could turn into self-absorbed snobbery. "Not him—his family. The police arrested Mr. Martin." Ginger dabbed her lips with a serviette. "And he isn't foul-smelling. Or old."

Lucy placed her toast on her plate and nodded emphatically. "Yes, he is. He smells like sauerkraut. All the time." Her eyes narrowed. "Is he a spy? Is that why they arrested him? I knew he must be. He always made me feel so uncomfortable. And I can hardly understand him."

Oh, for goodness' sake. Ginger rolled her eyes. She moved her attention toward her father, unwilling to entertain Lucy's ridiculous claims. "Will you be able to help the Martins?"

"Having the Martins stay here isn't possible. We must

close the house—it would be too expensive to keep it open while the family is in Cairo." Her father folded his newspaper and looked directly at Ginger. "But speaking of your mother and the Martins, she mentioned to me last night she wanted to go and call on Mrs. Martin today. Perhaps you'd be keen to accompany her."

"I would, thank you. Lucy, would you like to go, too?" Ginger met Henry's eyes, knowing he'd easily be able to see her laughter.

Henry chortled as Lucy shuddered.

"No, thank you!" Lucy raised her chin. "I can think of a thousand other ways I'd like to spend my morning. Next, you'll be asking me to go downstairs and help the cook."

As though a lesson in cooking wouldn't do them all a world of good right now. Ginger couldn't revile Lucy for that, though. Her own knowledge of the kitchen was nonexistent.

"Help the cook? You'd likely burn the house down." Henry gave her a pointed look. "But your governess might need to take you on some charity outings. You're turning into a proper snob."

At least someone had said it.

Lucy's formerly round and childish face was beginning to take a lovely shape, her cheekbones stronger. She was getting older. The gap in their ages had made it nearly impossible for them to be playmates—not to mention the time Ginger had spent away at finishing school. She'd hardly noticed Lucy growing up behind her and had often relegated her to being little more than a child. Maybe none of them had paid as much attention to Lucy's highbrow attitude as they should have.

* * *

GINGER BROUGHT her concerns about Lucy up with her mother as they rode into the village later that afternoon. "Mother, I wonder if Lucy isn't getting a little too wrapped up in this idea of finishing school and being out in society. She was in tears when father mentioned she might have a delay with the war."

A strand of her mother's red hair flew into her eyes and she tucked it away behind her ear. She smiled placidly. "Ginger, she's always admired you. And you've had so much success in London. I'm sure she wants to be like you."

"Success?" The hillsides were lush and Ginger imagined the sea in the distance and the spray of salt in the breeze. Penmore's proximity to the seaside made it a favorite for their extended family to come and visit in the summer months. While the rest of London was closing the Season and heading to hunts in Scotland and the North, they'd always left early to spend some time near the sea.

Not this year, though. Ginger sighed. Who knew when she could go sea-bathing next?

Her mother brought her mind back to the conversation. "Yes, you've had success whether you appreciate it or not." Lady Elizabeth folded her hands on her lap. "I take it you don't want to accept Stephen? Is there a reason you're so hesitant? You may come to love him."

"And I may never love him." The sun beat on her through the window, and she angled toward the shaded side of the car. "But it's more than that—there's something about Stephen which worries me. As much as you may like Lord Knotley and Rufus, Stephen is neither of those men. Even though Henry has always seen him like a brother, that's not reason enough for me to trust him. I can't put my finger on it, Mother. It's a feeling I don't quite understand myself."

"Well," her mother searched her gaze, "it's only natural for a woman to have some nerves about the prospect of marriage. Especially these days. But marriage isn't the prison some of those suffragettes would have you believe, either."

The implication that she objected to marriage instead of the prospective groom was maddening. Was it possible she'd allowed herself to become poisoned and prejudiced against Stephen without good reason? Her family seemed to disregard her concerns too easily. Her mind scrambled to help her explain herself better. "No, that's not it. I have this sense there should be something more to the whole thing. Excitement at the very least. But when I think of marrying Stephen, all I feel is dread. And father seems determined I should marry him no matter what I feel."

Her mother's lips bunched, revealing soft creases in the skin around her mouth. "Your father has financial considerations to keep in mind. Stephen has promised to give his financial help with Penmore. And your father has many concerns about the economy—especially now with the country at war."

Her father had implied as much, but it didn't help Ginger feel any more convinced about Stephen being right for her. She resented feeling like a disposable asset in a financial transaction. "But now that Henry's become so besotted with Angelica Fisher, shouldn't that match be enough for father to feel more secure about the future of Penmore?"

Her mother adjusted the scarf knot under her chin. "Yes, well, we all thought it would settle things when Henry asked for Charlotte Thompson's hand also, didn't we? Yet she threw away the chance to be a countess without thinking twice."

Charlotte's decision had stunned everyone—except for Ginger. The day Charlotte had met Robert, she'd practically glowed while telling Ginger about him. Her blue eyes had held a sparkle Ginger had never seen. *But won't your parents be furious?* Ginger had asked her.

"And what of it?" Charlotte had responded. *"We're expected to do nothing more than marry, but if that's going to be the sum of it, at the very least I'll marry whom I like. And who knows, maybe there'll be more to life besides calls, charity drives, and fashion afterward. Times are changing, after all."*

Charlotte's scathing critique of the life had left Ginger unsettled. Her depiction of the life of women in their circle was spot-on. Even child-rearing belonged to nannies and governesses. She stared at her gloved ring finger, thinking of the diamond Stephen had offered her. Charlotte's family had been furious, but they hadn't disinherited her either. But Charlotte was also an heiress.

In Ginger's case, the situation was less favorable. Henry would inherit. And even if Henry wasn't the oldest, the entail on the family's estate wouldn't allow her to inherit—only the closest male heir. Her best option was to marry well.

For once, though, Ginger wished she could do whatever her heart wanted. The only young man she'd ever been remotely interested in, Charles Wallace, had never even noticed her. She didn't want to remember her humiliation. Rather than being swept away by romance, she'd watched him pursue her cousin, Meg, who had rejected him.

Was she destined to forget the childish fantasy of true love?

She blinked away the old memories. "Charlotte had the freedom offered by her inheritance to choose whomever she wanted. I don't blame her for choosing love."

Her mother gave her a sympathetic smile. "You shouldn't let Charlotte's decision influence your own, then. You don't have the same luxuries."

Her mother's words weighed heavily on Ginger's heart. A burning feeling rose at the base of her throat. "But what if Charlotte chose wisely? She's happy, mother. The women campaigning for rights don't have everything quite right, but they raise valid questions. And I don't want to feel unduly forced to marry Stephen to ease Father's worries. It may have been the choice you had to make, but why should I have to do the same?"

Her mother's mouth dipped into a frown, displeasure shadowing her eyes. "If I had chosen differently, you wouldn't be here." She cleared her throat, clearly more annoyed by Ginger's comment than she wanted to verbalize.

Ginger forced her gaze on the passing blur of the landscape. Maybe she wasn't being fair to her mother, but she couldn't help it, either. Her mother had obviously been interested in the title and comfort her father had offered her in her youth. Neither of those things would tempt her to marry a man like Stephen.

After a few moments of tense silence, her mother said, "Your father also offered me something you seem to have overlooked. For all his flaws, your father has always treated me with respect. I could have done far worse than him."

"But what about better?" Ginger's voice was tight. "What about love? Didn't you ever dream of romance?"

"I didn't read as many novels as you do. Romance is often exaggerated in fiction. You'll find all romance fades in time. Looks fade, attraction disappears, and if you're lucky to be left with respect and comfort, you've done well. Yes, I may have had a few suitors who would have provided the excitement you seem to look for. But sacrificing that was a small price to pay for the life I have now. I'd trade nothing for my current life." Her mother reached over and patted her hand. "Let's not quarrel, darling. I trust in the end you'll make the best decision, not only for yourself but for the family."

Her mother's words didn't comfort Ginger.

Thankfully, the car drew to a stop in front of the Martins' shop. As Bosworth helped them step out, her mother turned toward Ginger. "Ginger, why don't you go down the road and buy a few loaves of bread from the bakery?" She lifted the basket the cook had packed from the seat of the car. "With as many children as Mrs. Martin has, she might need more than the cook sent. I'll go ahead in."

Ginger nodded, clasping her handbag. The conversation with her mother had left her feeling spent. She was grateful for the escape. As she approached the bakery, the sweet scent of yeast and baking bread filled the air. Ginger paused at the window of the shop. Baked goods enticed from the window, from sticky buns to long baguettes.

The bakery had the same thatched cottage style as so many of the buildings in town. Penmore offered an idyllic look into a world long-since passed. Though it wouldn't compare to the ancient feeling of a place like Cairo.

High-pitched shouts caught her attention. Across the street, in one of the open squares, a group of boys appeared to be playing. Ginger watched them, then her brow furrowed.

Not playing. *Fighting.*

She dashed across the street, drawing closer to the sound of their boisterous shouts. A group of children encircled two boys, no older than ten, who wrestled on the grass. "Get 'im," one boy in the circle whooped.

Of the two boys fighting, one was larger, with dark, tousled hair and broad shoulders. Dirt streaked his hands and forehead as he attempted to stuff grass in the mouth of the other child, a smaller boy with white-blond hair Ginger recognized from when he'd come with his father for deliveries. One of the Martin boys.

Her heart lurched. This had to be about Mr. Martin.

The Martin boy was bleeding from a cut on his temple, above his eye, his face as red as a strawberry. Ginger pushed through the circle of boys. "Stop!" She reached for the Martin boy, but the boy beating him knocked his elbow into her stomach by mistake.

Dropping back with a flash of pain, Ginger's anger rose as her hat tumbled onto the grass. "Stop this at once!" She searched the perimeter for any other adult face. A woman across the street pushing a pram had stopped and stared at them but didn't come forward.

The bully realized who he had hit and stood straight. He wiped his bleeding nose with the back of his hand, his eyes narrowed and menacing. "His father's a dirty Hun, my lady."

"And so you beat him?" Ginger caught her breath, her diaphragm aching from where the child had struck her. "What's your name? I have half a mind to drag you before the constable myself." She snatched her hat from the grass and dusted it off before replacing it.

"Archie Winser." The boy continued to glare at the Martin boy.

Ginger leveled her chin at him. He was the son of a local pig farmer who rented land from them. "Winser? Is that what you're calling yourselves these days? I'm quite sure I know of a Thomas Wissner who anglicized his name some years ago so it wouldn't sound too German. I'll let my father know what a beast his son is."

Archie's eyes widened, his cheeks and neck flushing as the other boys in the group exchanged suspicious looks. From the boy's reaction, he may not have known about his own background. She sucked in a quick, guilty breath between her teeth.

Ginger pulled the Martin boy up straight as the other boys dispersed, mumbling amongst themselves. "Let's take you home," she said.

They hurried across the street. "I'm sorry." The boy hiccupped, holding back quiet sobs.

Was he embarrassed?

"You have nothing to apologize for." Ginger dug through her handbag for a handkerchief. "Hold this to your cut. What's your name?"

"Charlie," the boy took in a shattered breath. He kept his gaze low.

As they hurried down the pavement, the recruitment posters posted to the sides of buildings seemed to shout. Kitchener's face, with its bold moustache and narrowed eyes, issued the command to join the war effort. But there were other posters—stirring fear, propaganda, accusations. Posters with watching eyes, condemnations of extravagant lifestyles.

She shivered and placed a hand on Charlie's shoulder. People spoke of changes. Her country seemed to have changed already. But what were they all becoming?

CHAPTER FIVE

Staring at the light reflecting from the top of her crystal wine glass, Ginger barely heard her father speaking to her until he repeated her name.

She lifted her gaze. Across the dinner table, her father adjusted his white tie and gave her a sharp glance. "Are you?" he asked.

"Forgive me." Ginger considered taking another spoonful of her pudding. A bite of something might give her a moment to compose herself better for her father. "I didn't hear you."

"Are you becoming political?" Her father's stern expression burned with disapproval.

"I hardly call it political to be concerned about the injustice I see." Ginger shifted in her evening gown, feeling the heat of her father's stare.

Henry chuckled. "Perhaps you should look through Father's dictionary to learn the meaning of the word." He sat straighter against the back of his dining room chair. "I'm astonished to hear you won't readily admit it."

Ginger set her lips into a firm line. Her brother's insistence on playing the neutral party to disagreements was beyond irritating. Especially when she could use an ally. A quick glance at the servants in the room checked her desire to call him on it. She'd tell him of her disappointment later when they were in private.

As though she sensed Ginger's feeling of isolation, her mother tilted her chin. Her diamond earrings sparkled as she turned toward her husband. "Darling, you should have seen poor Mrs. Martin. The woman is as distraught as Ginger suggested. And with good reason. Look what happened to the Martin boy today."

Her father didn't appear swayed. "A terrible situation. But the Martins are hardly the only ones dealing with this, Elizabeth. We can't very well go fighting for the release of every incarcerated German national in England—it would defeat the entire purpose of the law. And if we make too much noise about this, someone could paint us as being too interested in the plight of the Germans. And where would that put us?"

Was this why everyone seemed so reluctant to help? "I understand, but surely officials will see the special circumstances of the Martins. You know Mr. Martin—"

"But do I?" Her father set his spoon on his plate. "How can I reasonably vouch he's not a spy? I don't know him well. Not well enough to know what sort of activities he's involved in."

Much as Ginger hated to admit it, her father had a point. She bit her tongue. Her gut instincts told her Mr. Martin was harmless, but it wasn't as if her father could use Ginger's feelings as the basis to arrange the Mr. Martin's release.

Her mother tugged at the top of her long white gloves. "Your worries do you credit, my dear. We are at war, after all." Her green eyes met Ginger's. "But Ginger makes a valid point, as well. Your patronage should count for something with the Home Secretary. And even if the elder Mr. Martin has less of a case, I don't think it would be unreasonable to see what we can do for young John. Particularly if he agrees to volunteer for service. What better way to prove he's a true Englishman at heart?"

"Hear, hear. Obviously, Ginny's gained her political prowess from you, dearest Mother." Henry lifted his glass in a laughing toast toward his mother. He winked at Ginger. "Now I have rather a favor to ask of you. Will you please finish your dessert so we can all move into the drawing room? I've got to catch a train in the morning to join some fellows on a hunt in a few days. I'd like to turn in early."

"Far be it from me to keep you from your brandy. I like to eat with proper manners." Ginger allowed her features to relax into a wry grin. She couldn't begrudge Henry's attempts to lighten the mood. She'd been carrying on about the Martins as boorishly as Lucy had about the move to Cairo all day.

Lucy laughed and swished her long dark hair, which her maid had curled for dinner. "And you think you could be a social reformer? You're a member of the oppressive class who likes their hours-long, drawn-out dinners. Or in your case, half a day. There's never been anyone who eats more slowly."

Across the round table, her mother beamed at the three of them. "I'm glad to have a little sense of normalcy before we leave Penmore. I'll miss these times soon."

Lucy appeared stricken at the reminder.

"Leave it to you, dear Mama, to end the dinner on a somber note." Henry folded his serviette.

As they retired from the dining room, the truth of her mother's words filled Ginger with a sense of regret. Even if nothing changed in the coming war—which seemed an impossibility—her family expected her to marry soon. She reached out and ran her fingertips over the trim in the hall-way, the spaces she'd occupied without always appreciating their beauty. Would Penmore ever be her home again?

She'd almost reached the next room when a warm draft of air raised the hair on the back of her neck. Mr. Pierce stood at the front door. The butler wore a grim expression. Beyond him waited Charlie Martin.

Henry, who followed behind her, turned to see what she stared at. "What is it?" His gaze shot back to Ginger's.

"I don't know." Her eyes darted toward the drawing room where the rest of her family had entered. Charlie couldn't be here to bring good news. She set a gloved hand on Henry's forearm. "I'm going to go check."

Henry nodded. "I'll come with you."

Henry reached the door first. "I'll take the lad from here, Pierce."

Ginger set her hands on Charlie's shoulders. The boy heaved for breath. "What is it? Did you run here?"

Charlie nodded, a bead of sweat trickling down his red face. "Mum sent me here because I'm the fastest. It's that—someone threw a brick through the window. And there was a note." The boy's hands trembled as he handed it to Ginger.

Ginger uncrumpled the dirty sheet of paper, which was damp with sweat. The scrawled handwriting appeared hastily written, large looping letters warning of a coming attack. A tight feeling encircled her heart. *Oh no.* She slipped the paper quietly to Henry, trying to remain calm. "Do you know who threw the brick?"

Charlie shook his head. "No, but Mum thinks Mr. Winser is behind it."

"The pig farmer?" Henry asked.

"Mum thinks he's angry with what Lady Virginia said."

Had she done something wrong? Ginger swallowed her

astonishment as Henry shot her a quizzical look. "Pierce—" Henry called out.

Mr. Pierce came from around the corner.

"—can you please fetch this young lad some water? And stay with him. We'll return in a moment." Henry grabbed Ginger by the elbow and pulled her from the entrance toward the library. Once inside, he demanded, "What did you do?"

Ginger shook her head, her long dangling earrings feeling heavy in her ears with the movement. "I don't know—I..." She thought back to the fight. "Charlie was fighting with the Winser boy and I stopped it. And when the boy told me his name, I checked his pride by telling him I knew his own father had changed their name from Wissner..."

"What?" Henry's voice boomed. "Well, no wonder the man is furious. It's a wonder he's not throwing bricks through the windows of Penmore."

Why was he reacting so furiously? Ginger shrank back. "But I don't understand—"

"Darling sister—Thomas Winser changed his name years ago to avoid the German association. You claim to be concerned about the plight of good Englishmen who are being discriminated against. Think about what you've done." Henry opened the door. "Pierce, tell Bosworth to pull the car around at once."

Setting a hand over her parted mouth, Ginger stared at the scowl on Henry's face. *He's right.*

"Damn it, Ginny. This time you may have gone too far by being careless with your words. Your impulsivity is bound to catch up with you."

She didn't try to defend herself. How could she have been so stupid?

"You think Thomas Winser means to retaliate against the Martins in order to prove his loyalty to England?"

Henry's jaw clenched and his eyes became slits as he nodded. "He's also likely furious you've publicized his own Germanic background. Honestly, Ginny, what were you thinking? He may try to retaliate against you or the family." The heels of Henry's well-shined shoes clapped against the marble flooring in the foyer as he strode back toward Charlie.

Bile crept up her throat.

What have I done?

She had been so smug. So satisfied with herself.

Stupid, ignorant fool.

Ginger fled after Henry. "Where are you going?"

"Mrs. Martin and her children need our immediate aid." He glanced at the butler, then back at her. "I'm going to the village. Don't interrupt Mama and Papa yet to tell them where I've gone. They can wonder where I've gone off to for a bit, but I don't want to worry them needlessly. With any luck, the threat to the Martins will come to nothing."

"I'm going with you." Her parents would notice they'd gone immediately, but if Pierce said nothing for a few minutes, it gave her the leverage she needed to slip away with Henry. Ginger pulled her earrings off and then slipped her necklace over her head. "Mr. Pierce, please give these to Violet to replace in my bedroom."

"My lady, is it wise for you to go? It's late." Pierce took the jewelry from her, but looked over the top of her head toward Henry.

"I'll be fine." She motioned toward Charlie. "Come on. Let's take you back home."

"I don't think—" Henry began.

Ginger silenced him with a sharp look. "If I created this, the very least you can allow me to do is to fix it." She counted on Henry's dislike of quarreling to help convince him.

Henry's nod was clipped.

Together with Henry and Charlie, she rushed out into the summer night. The air held the slightest chill, reminding her they were heading steadily away from long days of festivity. Her ankles wobbled in the driveway's gravel. She wished she'd changed into something more suitable—an evening gown with fine beads seemed cumbersome at nearly nine in the evening. If she ripped anything, Violet would have her work cut out for her to put it all back together.

Within a few minutes, Bosworth had brought the car around. They jostled down the driveway toward the village, dust from the gravel pluming behind them. On the leather seat beside her, Charlie radiated heat which matched his rapid pulse. An earthy, unwashed scent rose from his skin.

Ginger met Henry's eyes in the seat across from hers. Henry said nothing, but she read the concern in his expression. He wouldn't have rushed off like this if he didn't think the threat to the Martins was credible. Or that it could show up on their doorstep.

She should have been wiser than to say what she'd said about Thomas Winser. Holding her tongue was often a skill she'd lacked as a child—though her governess had done her best to drill it out of her.

But when she remembered Archie Winser's smug look as he'd stared down poor Charlie, her anger resurfaced. How easy it was for Archie to cast stones. Though he was quite young. She'd had the impression he hadn't even known about his own family background—breaking the news to him must have been a blow.

As they drew closer to the village, the moonlight highlighted the whites of Henry's eyes. Ginger reached across the car for his hand, the pressure of nerves battering her insides. Henry leaned forward and took her hand in his. His hands were warm and steady, with the sort of confidence she'd always loved about him. Even when she was a girl, he'd been the first to offer her comfort in the face of fear.

After they'd first arrived at Penmore from Cairo when she was younger, she'd refused to sleep in the nursery. Her Egyptian governess had often told her frightening fairy tales and parables to keep her in line, and Ginger had become convinced a ghost haunted the nursery. She'd sneak to Henry's room when fear got the better of her—and he always allowed her to sleep curled up against him. She'd find herself back in the nursery by morning, another favor.

Moonlight outlined the Martins' house, the thatched roof absorbing the light. They were nearly there when Henry let go of her hand and pivoted toward the chauffer. "Go around to the other side."

Ginger's eyes darted toward Charlie. She left him on the seat they'd occupied, scooting across to join Henry. "What is it?"

Henry's eyes remained focused outside the car. He leaned back, unblinking. "I'm certain I saw someone by the gate." He lowered his voice. "I shouldn't have brought you. Father will have my head if I put you in harm's way. I'll have Bosworth leave me and then take you directly back to Penmore. I sense trouble. Foolish of me not to have brought a pistol."

A pistol?

Horror cut her from belly to sternum.

What was it Henry thought he had seen? She didn't want to cause Charlie any more alarm than necessary, but Henry's plan seemed absurd. "For God's sake, I won't ride merrily back home while you may be in danger. If it makes things better, I'll stay in the car with Charlie while you speak to Mrs. Martin."

Bosworth slowed the car and pulled it to a stop. He stepped out and opened the door for Henry. "Stay here." Henry pointed a finger at the inside of the car.

Ginger fidgeted in her seat as Henry's figure disappeared around the corner. She'd made a mess of things. She gave the little boy a tight smile, but he was busy staring outside.

A loud crack, like a gunshot, startled them both. Charlie jumped up and then pushed open the car door. He scrambled in the direction Henry had gone.

Stumbling against the door, Ginger bumped her way out of the backseat. Her feet hit the pavement. She steadied herself against the frame of the car.

"No, my lady!" Bosworth bolted from his seat.

"I'll be fine, Bosworth. Stay with the car." Ginger ran, trying to keep Charlie in her sight. With the boy being faster and small, he was already far ahead of her. And it was dark. Within a few moments, he disappeared around the corner.

She reached the back gate to the Martins' property out of breath. She felt for the latch on the gate, the fabric of her glove catching on a thorn from a rosebush. The thorn pricked her finger. The wound throbbed, and she yanked her hand back. Pinching her fingertip in the fist of her other hand, she pushed the gate open with her hip.

The goat. She shuddered.

She hastened down the path toward the back door where she'd called on Mrs. Martin the day before. Her knock provoked whispered voices, then the door opened a crack. Henry peeked out. He threw the door open more widely. "What in the bloody hell are you doing here?"

His language and fury rendered her speechless.

Henry yanked her in and slammed the door closed behind her. His hands curled into fists. "I told you to stay in the car."

Ginger struggled to find her voice. She couldn't remember many times Henry had ever been this angry with her. "I followed Charlie. We heard something and then he tore out of the car."

Mrs. Martin, who had been standing a few steps behind Henry, rushed forward. "Charlie isn't with you?"

Several children sat on a small, ragged sofa. Charlie wasn't among them. Ginger took two steps further into the house, her diaphragm dropping low as dread crept into her stomach. "He's not here?" The room, stuffy and hot, seemed to suffocate.

Mrs. Martin's face paled. "Charlie!" She turned toward the narrow staircase leading upstairs. "Charlie!" Her voice sounded panicked. She wrung her apron in her hands before rushing up the stairs.

If Charlie wasn't here, where had he gone? He knew this area better than she did. Maybe he had a secret hiding place or a safer way into the house.

A knot formed in the pit of her stomach. Unless someone had stopped him. Wouldn't she have noticed?

Henry lifted his hat, wiping sweat from his forehead with a handkerchief. "Tell Mrs. Martin to pack her most valuable things and bring them with her. Then help her and the children back to the car. I'm going out to look for Charlie. Don't wait for me. Take them to Penmore without me. I'll find my way back once I find Charlie."

Henry slipped out the door. Without Henry or Mrs. Martin to talk to, Ginger turned her attention to the other Martin children. Five faces stared at her—four girls and one baby boy, no older than a year. They were small, but would they all even fit in the car? The oldest girl, about Lucy's age, held the baby in her arms, her golden hair in tidy braids on either side of her face.

"Can you pack a bag for your siblings?" Ginger met her light blue eyes. The girl appeared fearful, but calm.

"Me what, miss?

"I mean for yourself and all the other children."

She nodded and held the baby out toward one of her sisters, who appeared to be a few years younger than her.

"It may be faster if you both do it. I can hold the baby if you'd like." Ginger came closer to them.

The two girls exchanged a look and then examined Ginger's dress. Ginger shifted, feeling more unsuitably dressed than before. The money she'd spent on this dress was probably more than the Martins used to clothe all their children.

Ginger held out her hands. "It's all right. You go on."

The older girl handed Ginger the baby and curtsied. She took her sister by the hand and went up the stairs.

The baby in Ginger's arms squirmed, swiveling his head to stare at her face. He reached out with chubby fingers toward her jaw, pawing at her clumsily. She smiled at him, but he felt awkward in her hands—not at all like she'd imagined holding a baby would be like.

Of course, she'd never held a baby.

The baby stared at her, unblinking, the concern in his eyes growing, his tiny face scrunching as his lip quivered. A sharp, ear-piercing squeal followed as he cried, his entire face turning red.

Ginger held him away from her body. Perhaps she'd gotten too close.

She turned, scanning the faces of the other children, but they were toddlers.

Relief filled her as Mrs. Martin's footsteps sounded behind her. She took the baby in her arms. He calmed immediately. "Charlie's not in the house." She bounced the baby against her hip.

"My brother went out after him. He told me to tell you to gather your valuables and come with us to Penmore. I sent the older girls to pack a bag."

"Thank you, my lady." She lifted a trembling hand to her forehead. "I don't understand why this is happening."

At least Mrs. Martin had the courtesy not to make Ginger feel worse about the incident with Archie Winser. Ginger cringed. "I'm so sorry—"

Mrs. Martin's eyes widened as though she believed she had offended Ginger. "I didn't mean that, my lady. I meant to my family. My husband is a good man."

Every day, the atrocities the German soldiers committed against the Belgian citizens filled the newspapers. As much as she sympathized with the Martins, Ginger understood why her countrymen were furious with the Germans. She shared their anger. But what was happening to the Martins was unconscionable. "The awful truth is I fear it's only going to become worse the more we're drawn into this war. The news from Belgium is frightful. Is there anyone else in town you can trust, Mrs. Martin?"

Mrs. Martin cradled her baby closer. "They're all afraid. I'll go and pack a handbag with some things."

"We should hurry. Henry seemed under the impression someone was watching the front of the shop."

Mrs. Martin took only minutes to return with a bag no larger than a book. Her daughters came down the stairs with her, carrying a small suitcase. Ginger helped them extinguish the oil lamps in the room before they all hurried outside.

"This way." Ginger kept her voice low as they went down the path leading to the gate. They'd gone only a few steps when the crashing sound of glass shattering behind them made Ginger jump.

Mrs. Martin whirled around toward the house, horror on her face. "The shop!" She hugged her baby closer.

The smell of smoke reached Ginger before she saw flames shooting from the top of the roof. Her heart pounded. Who would do such a thing? "Hurry!" Ginger lifted one of the smaller girls nearest to her. "Hurry, Mrs. Martin!"

They fled past the gate. Ginger felt a sharp pinch in her ankle as she twisted it. She ignored the pain, her grip tight on the little girl. Each step ached, her teeth grinding as she led the Martin children forward. "Quickly, quickly now!"

The car wasn't far, but somehow the distance felt longer than when she'd followed Charlie. Fear clawed at her. She had the unmistakable feeling they were being watched and followed.

Would someone really attack a woman fleeing with her children?

Ginger shivered. Or her? Many of the villagers benefited from the Braddock estate. Surely, they wouldn't attack.

If they could even recognize her this time of night.

As they neared the car, Bosworth rushed to her aid. "Lady Virginia, please hurry into the car." He took the child from her and helped her step inside. Mrs. Martin and her children followed, the space quickly becoming crowded. A few of the children sat on the floor. Ginger settled the little girl she'd carried onto the seat, then stepped back out of the car.

"Henry said not to wait for him," Ginger told Bosworth. He nodded and jumped into his seat.

Ginger stared at their pale white faces, the terror in their innocent, wide eyes. They breathed heavily, shoulder to shoulder. Mrs. Martin stared out the window toward her home. The reddish haze of flames filled the dark night.

Pinning her arms against her stomach, Ginger backed away from the car slowly. She closed the door to the car, the scent of petrol stinging her eyes. She could be to blame for this.

Bosworth turned toward her. "My lady?"

She swallowed hard. "Go on ahead, Bosworth. I'll be along with Henry."

"No, my lady, I can't leave—"

Giving him a stern look, she leveled her chin. "Go. Henry asked me to go and find him."

The struggle on Bosworth's face was evident. He clearly didn't want to leave her—fearing the wrath of her father—but he also didn't want to contradict her or Henry's orders.

At last, he gave a nod. As the car tore away from the village, Ginger's hands relaxed from tight fists. She turned sharply and rushed back toward the burning house. Her ankle throbbed now. Shouts sounded on the side of the house facing the main street. By now, the fire had stirred neighbors. Some stood at their back doorsteps, gawking at the conflagration.

Ginger rushed back to the gate. She'd have to run around the block rather than go by the side of the house. A head butted the gate, giving it a shake. The goat. Poor creature was probably terrified.

Going through the gate, Ginger found a rope. She looped it around the goat's neck and tied a knot. Pulling, she tried to help it through the gate. It didn't budge. Thick smoke and ash filled the air.

"My lady!" a voice came from nowhere. One neighbor had rushed from his back door. He held out his hand for the rope. "I'll take care of the goat. You shouldn't be here!"

Glad to be rid of the animal, Ginger handed over its care. She lifted her skirts as she hastened around the block toward the main street of town. With each step, the pain in her ankle grew worse. She limped her way forward. The ringing of the fire engine bell clanged, followed by the clopping of horses' hooves. As the wagon pulling the water pump drew closer, Ginger searched the street for any sign of Henry or Charlie. A crowd had gathered by now, watching the spectacle.

Sickness clawed at her throat. She had wanted to help the Martins, not cause the destruction of their home.

A boy approached down the street, looking over his shoulder at the fire. He turned away, then stopped short when he saw her. *Archie Wisner.*

Their eyes met. Archie bolted.

"Wait!" Ginger called. *Drat.* A flash of white-hot pain shot through her as she dashed to follow him, her ankle screaming. He might know what had happened to Charlie. He'd taken off at a full sprint, down a lane.

The darkness of the lane swallowed him. Her footsteps faltered. Archie's father had every reason to be angry with her. If he was behind the fire and the brick, she could be in danger.

Images of Mrs. Martin clutching her baby to her played through her mind. No mother should ever have to leave her house in terror like that. Especially when Mrs. Martin had done nothing wrong.

She had to help Henry find Charlie. Archie Wisner might be the best way to do that.

Her heels struck the pavement with loud clacks as she pushed herself forward. Her safety wasn't important compared to Charlie's. He was just a boy.

The lane emptied into a dirt road, and past it was a public house. She didn't see Archie anywhere. The area around the left side of the public house had shabby stalls for horses. Had he hidden there? Ginger drew closer, then froze as the stalls came into view. Three rough-looking men had gathered in there. They hovered over a recumbent form on the straw-covered floor of the stall. Muffled crying greeting her ears.

Charlie.

She rushed into their midst. The boy lay bruised and battered, blood soaking his pants. The man closest to Charlie held a piece of lead pipe in his hands. They turned toward Ginger with menacing looks.

"It'd be best if you go," the man with the lead piping said, his voice cold.

"What have you done?" Ginger pushed her way toward Charlie, but another man grabbed her arm. "Let me go." She yanked herself free, trying to get to him, then slapped the man restraining her.

He shoved her away. She fell on the straw with a cry, her backside hitting the ground hard. The fall had done no favors to the ache in her ankle, either. She gawked at them. In the dark, she couldn't recognize them or distinguish their features well. They had to know who she was from the manner of her dress, though—didn't they?

Then again, announcing her name might not help her right now if they didn't. Not if she'd caused this.

Charlie moaned beside her, his little hand trembling as he reached for her. The man with the club lifted it, as though to knock his hand away.

Her heart slammed against her ribcage. "No!" She threw herself over the boy. "Stay away from this child." The smell of horse manure was cloying

"Stop!" Henry's familiar voice boomed through the space. Relief pulsed through her at the sight of him. His white tie garments were in stark contrast to the setting, but they gave him an air of authority. At the sight of Henry, the man's companions backed away, fear on their faces. They turned and ran away.

The man with the lead pipe whirled toward Henry. "You might be a spy, too, Whitman. Ye're willin' to betray England to the bloody Huns." Rather than backing away, he charged toward Henry, knocking him off his feet. The two men tumbled to the ground. A scuffle of groans and sickening punches between them followed. Ginger shielded Charlie for a moment longer, scanning the perimeter for some tool to help Henry.

Spotting a rake, she dove toward it. Ginger stumbled to her feet, straw sticking to her skirt. Her hands wrapped around the handle of the rake. She turned it flat side out. Whirling it toward the attacker, she struck his back.

The man grunted and fell forward. The distraction was enough for Henry to scramble away, heaving with deep breaths.

Moments later, the attacker was on his feet again, running away.

Ginger's knees weakened as the attacker disappeared. Unsteadily, she approached Henry. "Are you all right?"

In the pale moonlight, his expression was haggard. Scrapes and cuts marred his face and hands and his lower lip was swollen and split. He dabbed at his lip with his fingertips, then pulled her into his arms. "I could murder you for being here, but thank you."

"I-I…" Relief overcame her. *Thank goodness he's all right.* She took a shattered breath, then pulled herself away. "Charlie—they hurt him."

Henry approached Charlie with caution. The boy continued to moan and shake. "My leg—" he managed.

"It must have been the same lot that torched the Martins' shop," Henry said, crouching beside the boy. He winced at the dark pool of blood under his leg. Slipping his arms under Charlie's thighs and back, he lifted the boy, causing the boy to scream. "Let's get him to Dr. Morgan."

The cottage hospital wasn't a long walk. But for the first time in her life, Ginger feared being in the village. She followed Henry closely. "They attacked us," she said, partially to herself.

"They did." Henry squinted in the darkness. His words told her nothing about his thoughts. Was he still angry with her for all of this? For as much as was happening in the village at this late hour, they were alone. Surely people had heard Charlie—his cries were enough to provoke curiosity. But it was as though others felt they shouldn't interfere.

They arrived at the cottage hospital. Ginger removed her glove and rapped on the door with the heavy knocker. Within minutes, a shuffle sounded as the lock turned. The door opened and Dr. Morgan stood there.

He gaped at them, the glow of a yellow electric bulb behind him. Ginger had only met the man once—he'd replaced the former physician in the village late in April. "Two men with burns, a woman in labor. What now?" The annoyance in his voice was thick.

"It's one of the Martin children," Henry said, lifting the boy just slightly. "They've attacked him."

"Come in." Dr. Morgan held the door for them. He gave Ginger an odd look. She touched the back of her head. Straw stuck out from her hair and to her dress.

She brushed away the straw on the step, then followed Henry and Dr. Morgan into the hospital.

He led them into an examination room and switched the light on. Henry set Charlie on the table. The boy shrieked as his leg met the hard surface.

Ginger leaned into the door frame, hanging back. In the light, she saw more than she'd been able to before. The bone below Charlie's kneecap jutted out from the skin and fabric of his torn pants.

She grimaced.

Dr. Morgan cut the fabric of his pants away, revealing the gruesome injury further. Charlie howled, and Ginger stepped further in. She gripped the boy's hand and offered a soothing hush. "It's all right, sweet boy. Hold my hand tight," she whispered. She mopped up his tears with a handkerchief.

The attacker had bludgeoned Charlie's kneecap, breaking the bone. Dr. Morgan's lips set in a grim line as he leaned closer, inspecting the wound. His touches were light, but even the slightest pressure seemed to provoke screams from the boy.

Straightening, Dr. Morgan nodded at Henry. "Follow me."

Henry did as Dr. Morgan had asked him. Eager to hear what the doctor had to say, Ginger pressed the handkerchief into Charlie's hand. "I'll be right back," she said, before rushing to follow them.

Dr. Morgan shut the door to the examination room. The closed door did little to diminish the sounds of Charlie's cries. He turned to them. "I'd like to speak to the boy's father." He checked his pocket watch. "I have little time. I must go to check on the laboring mother."

"The boy's father isn't available," Ginger said. She hesitated to say more. Who knew how Dr. Morgan felt about the Martins? Her willingness to trust in the goodwill of the people in the town had serious limits.

An impatient look crossed Dr. Morgan's face. "Then I'll need to speak to the mother."

"I can go and fetch her." Henry put a soothing hand on Ginger's shoulder. "My sister will stay with the boy in the meantime. May I borrow your telephone to call my driver?"

"Can you give the boy something for his pain?" Ginger asked as Dr. Morgan moved to lead Henry away.

He scratched his forehead. "I can sedate him. I'll return shortly."

As Henry and the doctor walked away, Ginger let herself back into the room. Charlie's eyes were wild as he pivoted his head toward the door. "I want my mum." Fat tears ran down his cheeks, his face red. "I want my mum."

Ginger was at his side and wiped the tears from his face, her heart heavy with guilt. His mother needed to be here. She would be the only one who could console him. But who would console the other frightened children she'd have to leave behind to come here? "She's on her way,

Charlie. We're going to make sure you're taken care of, I promise."

Without Dr. Morgan or Henry in the room, disquiet crept into her heart. The image of the man hovering over her with a lead pipe made her startle. Had Henry not arrived, what might he have done? She'd been foolish to go on her own. She'd been too trusting.

The people in this village had known her since she was a child. They'd celebrated at events thrown by her parents. Benefited from her family's charity.

They had still attacked her and Henry.

As she held onto the sobbing child, her promise to help him felt hollow to her own ears. Had she done anything at all to help the Martins...or had she only made things worse?

CHAPTER SIX

*M*rs. Martin arrived shortly after Charlie drifted to sleep from the medicine the doctor had given him. A sick feeling still clenched at the back of Ginger's throat. She unclasped her hand from Charlie's, noticing the blood sticking her fingers to his.

Her parents were behind Mrs. Martin, still dressed for dinner.

Ginger rose to her feet, with a mixture of relief and apprehension at their arrival. "Thank goodness you're here," she said as Mrs. Martin rushed to Charlie's side.

Charlie opened his eyes drowsily, his face no longer bunched with pain. "Mum," he whispered, reaching for her.

Mrs. Martin tearfully took his hand, then drooped beside him as she saw his injury.

Her father caught her arm and helped her to the chair. "Where's the doctor?" he asked Ginger.

"He's tending to a woman in labor but promised to return shortly." Ginger smoothed her hands over her skirt. The examination room felt full now with them all crowded inside it. Henry was noticeably absent. "Where's Henry?"

"We dropped him by the police to speak to the authorities about the events of this evening. He'll be along shortly," her father said. He had yet to meet Ginger's gaze, which spoke volumes. More than likely, Henry had told her father about Ginger's part in all this. He would be as furious with her as Henry had been.

Ginger approached her mother. "Can we speak in the vestibule, Mama?"

They exited the room, leaving her father with Mrs. Martin. Ginger led her mother away from the doorway. She winced at the pain in her ankle, digging her fingernails into the palms of her hands. Telling her mother about her ankle would only worry her parents more. "Were the Martins able to settle into the house? Who's with the children?"

"We left them in the old nursery with some servants. They're frightened, but fine. For now." Her mother wore a serious expression.

"What do you mean, 'for now?'"

Her mother took her by the elbow. Her pupils were wide in the dim light, making her appear more stern. "Ginger, you never should have left Penmore tonight without telling us what had happened." She held out a hand to cut off any defense Ginger may interrupt with. "Don't worry, I'm just as upset with Henry. Your father and I know how deeply you feel about the plight of the Martins, and we, too, sympathize with them."

The door to the hospital opened and Dr. Morgan came inside. He nodded a greeting to them and then hurried into the examination room. Ginger didn't want to hear what she was certain would follow. "But what?"

Her mother covered Ginger's free hand with hers. "But we must be careful. Very careful. It'll do the whole family—not to mention your father's position with the government—a great deal of harm if we're seen as being pro-German."

Ginger tried to maintain her composure, exhausted from this struggle. "I hardly think housing an innocent woman and her children is a pro-German stance."

"Unfortunately, there are many who won't see things quite the same way as you do."

The words of the man who had attacked Henry came back to her. *"You might be a spy, too, Whitman. Ye're willin' to betray England to the bloody Huns."*

Boring her gaze into her mother's, Ginger narrowed her eyes. "Are you one of those who doesn't see things my way?"

"No, of course not." A line appeared between her mother's eyebrows, and she pursed her lips. She reached over and cupped Ginger's chin in her hand, her fingertips cool against Ginger's flushed skin. "But you're young, darling. You don't understand how cruel this world can be. Our circles would quickly ban your father if they felt his loyalties were in question."

Surely her mother had to be exaggerating. Besides being a member of the peerage, her father had spent his life in service to the Crown. "So we're to do nothing? We can't very well cast Mrs. Martin and her children out, Mother. She has nowhere to go. And the village is dangerous for her. This evening more than proved that."

"Yes, yes, I know." She sighed, looking back at the closed examination room door with agitation. "Your father and I will discuss it further. Don't worry, we won't be throwing them onto the street. We must find a solution that also doesn't cause our family harm. We may try putting them up somewhere. Perhaps in another town where no one knows them."

A woman's cry came from the examination room. Exchanging a glance, Ginger and her mother rushed to the door. Mrs. Martin stood by her son, a handkerchief in her hands. Her father continued to hold onto her arm as though the woman might suddenly be unwell again.

"Y-you can't t-take his leg," Mrs. Martin said, her words choked by tears. She shook her head, her face a deep red.

Her father shifted with discomfort beside the crying woman. Ginger relieved him of the position. "Mrs. Martin, what's happened?"

"I've informed Mrs. Martin the boy's injuries are too severe. His leg will have to be amputated," Dr. Morgan said without a trace of gentleness. "He'll be fine. He'll live. And that's all that matters, really."

Ginger's lips parted in horror. The thought of poor Charlie being left a cripple by this was more than she could bear. "Isn't there some other option to reset his leg?"

Dr. Morgan released another sigh, then checked his pocket watch. "The extent of the injury would require the skills of a masterful surgeon. While I can do some surgeries here, I'm not equipped to handle something of this nature. Not to mention, you're speaking of options for the rich, Lady Virginia."

Mrs. Martin gripped Ginger's hand so tightly it hurt. "But...my boy. My poor boy. We rely on his help. And he's such a fast runner. Lives for it. He would climb and skip all day if he could. Please. Please help him. Don't cut off his leg."

Her father watched Mrs. Martin with a thoughtful expression. Displays of emotion made him uncomfortable, but he had a good heart. Perhaps, if there was hope, Ginger could convince him to step in on the boy's behalf. "Do you know someone who could do the surgery?" Ginger asked Dr. Morgan.

"Not here." Dr. Morgan scratched the top of his head. "Not anywhere near here, either. I have a friend in London but—"

"We'll take him to London, then. If that's all right with

you, Papa? I'm certain Mrs. Martin and I could take him." Ginger drew herself to her full height. She'd never live with herself if she didn't do everything in her power to save Charlie's leg.

"The trip for him will be excruciating. Not to mention he could die." Dr. Morgan held out a hand as though to put an end to her pleas. "And I can't guarantee they'll save his leg." He gave Mrs. Martin a severe look. "There's nothing wrong with being a cripple. Better a cripple than dead. Be reasonable for God's sake."

Ginger bristled at his condescension. "But the options aren't just dead or crippled, are they, Dr. Morgan? The right surgeon might save the leg."

"Yes, but—those are not the options for children like Charlie Martin," Dr. Morgan said, his face a mask of indifference.

Options for the rich. Insufferable man. Wasn't he supposed to do everything in his power to help and to heal?

"And if my family will help with the transport and cost?" Ginger avoided her parents' gazes. She should defer to them, as it was their motorcar and money she was offering, but she didn't want to look weak in front of Dr. Morgan.

Mrs. Martin appeared anguished by the situation. She appealed to Ginger's mother, who had been silent by the doorway. "What would you do, my lady?"

Her mother paled. She gave Mrs. Martin a kind smile. "I understand wanting to give one's child the best of options. Edmund, what do you think? Can we help take poor Charlie to London?"

Her father rubbed his jaw slowly. "If that's the desire of the mother, I'm happy to help."

"Oh, thank you, thank you, my lord. My whole family owes you so much." Mrs. Martin drew a shattered breath as she reached for Charlie's limp hand.

"This is ludicrous. Injuries of this nature result in amputation regularly." Dr. Morgan set his hands on his hips. "If you go, I wash my hands entirely of this. It makes no difference to me. I have enough patients to tend to for the evening, but I won't have others saying I put you up to this madness. I have my—"

Her father cut him off with a severe frown. "What's the name of the fellow in London, Morgan?"

"Dr. James Clark. At St. Thomas' Hospital. We trained together," Dr. Morgan said with a resigned look. He appeared to realize he had crossed too far of a line by challenging the Earl of Braddock. "I suppose I can put the boy's leg in a splint to keep his movement minimal while you move him. But you'll have to go tonight. Immediately."

Thank God.

Ginger had never felt such hopefulness and apprehension all at once.

Now she needed to convince her father to let her go with Charlie and Mrs. Martin to London. She'd made this catastrophe. She was determined to fix it.

"Why don't we speak of the arrangements in the hall while Dr. Morgan takes care of the splint? Mrs. Martin, you'll be all right, won't you?" her mother said.

With the way Dr. Morgan was behaving, Ginger worried more about leaving the beleaguered woman with him than anything else.

Mrs. Martin nodded mutely and they left her in the examination room.

A jittery feeling ran up Ginger's arms and she tried to keep her limp to a minimum. *One step at a time.* She breathed, clenching her jaw as she walked. What on earth had she done to her ankle?

They'd just made their way to the vestibule when Henry came through the front door. A bare bulb illuminated the space, but it made his face look even more haggard, especially because of his bruised face. He'd untied his bowtie and it hung around his neck. Closing the door, he sighed. "What does the doctor have to say?"

"He wants to amputate the boy's leg. Your sister has argued on behalf of the mother to send the boy to a surgeon in London who may repair the bone." Her father clasped his hands behind his back. "I've given my consent. Would you care to escort the boy to London?"

"I'd like to go," Ginger said, her tone flat. She didn't want there to be any argument.

Her father shifted, his brow furrowing. "To London?"

"You can't possibly go to London at this hour," her mother said. She set a steady hand on Ginger's forearm.

Henry winced, walking his fingertips over his swollen lip. An ugly purple bruise covered his cheek. "Mama is right, Ginny. Things are uncertain enough right now. It's best for you to be home. Not to mention the fact that I've accused the men involved with the police."

Ginger shook her head. "I'm certain it would be a comfort to Mrs. Martin for me to go with her to London."

Her father frowned. "I'm afraid she won't be able to go to London at all. And neither should you."

The soft buzz of the electric bulb pulsed in the tense air between them. Ginger readied herself for a clash with her father, anger coiling in the taut muscles of her arms. "And why won't she be able to go to London?"

Her father's gaze sliced toward her, as though she'd tried his patience enough. "Because of the Act." His tone held exasperation. "She's had to register as an enemy alien. She can't travel further than five miles from the village. Penmore is at the edge of where she might go, to be honest."

His words caught her off guard. She had expected him to say something about how he didn't really want to drive Mrs.

Martin to London or oversee the boy's care. How she'd over-stepped by offering. Now Ginger felt ignorant.

She'd buy an armful of newspapers in the morning and read everything about the blasted Act.

"You should stay here, Ginny." Henry sat on a settee, pain written on his features. "The trip to London could be diffi-cult for the boy. It might be frightening to witness."

Difficult or not, she had to help. She'd put Charlie and the Martins in further danger. Throwing her shoulders back, she said, "Did I balk at his injury? I was fine. I'm not a frail flower, Henry. And if Mrs. Martin can't go, then there's room enough for us both to accompany the boy."

Her mother crossed her arms. "It's too dangerous for you, Ginger. The men who did this to Charlie—and attacked Henry—could return. Or stop the car."

Please don't take their side, Mama. Without one ally, she might not go. "Then it's as dangerous for Henry, isn't it? No one is going to stop us on the way to London and ask if they have accused us of German sympathies." She swiveled her gaze to her father. "Please, Father. It'll give me a chance to check in with Stephen in London. See if he's made any progress with Home Secretary McKenna."

Mentioning Stephen was a trump card, and she didn't doubt her father would know why she'd used it. But it would also give him reason to hope she'd accept Stephen while in London.

Her father's dark eyes reflected a quickness that showed she was right. "And where will you stay? Morgan says the boy needs to leave immediately."

"With Madeline. She won't mind." Ginger's aunt was still in London for the end of the Season.

Her father gave her mother a surprised look, as though he hadn't expected Ginger to be so prepared with a response. "I don't need another one of my children injured over this."

"I promise I'll be careful." Ginger leaned forward and kissed his cheek. "Is that a yes?"

Her father scanned her face warily and nodded. "I know exactly what you're doing. Perhaps you'll consent to please me and come back an engaged woman."

Ginger stepped back from him and raised her chin. Even in the middle of the night and during calamity, her father didn't miss the opportunity to pressure her. Still, it would do her no good to seem stubborn and hard-headed. "You never know. Perhaps being in London again will inspire me to settle the issue once and for all."

A mildly pleased expression filled her father's face.

Ginger pressed her lips together. *Once and for all* could mean many things. She hoped her choice wouldn't estrange her from her father. Somehow, it felt as though the war had already fractured her world.

"Very good. You will need to drop us and Mrs. Martin off at Penmore after we've loaded the child. Hopefully Bosworth won't mind your mother and I squeezing in with him in the front."

Dr. Morgan and Henry transported Charlie to the idling motorcar on a stretcher, Mrs. Martin following. She wrung her hands as they walked out of the hospital. She turned to Ginger. "Thank you, Lady Virginia. For all you've done for me." She climbed in beside her son.

As Dr. Morgan exited from the car, he wore a scowl. He turned to Ginger. "Since this was your brilliant idea, I entrust the boy to you. If he grows pale or his pulse drops, I advise you to stop and find the closest doctor you can. Get him amputated if that happens."

Ginger's throat went dry. "How do I know if his pulse drops?"

The doctor reached for her hand. At her hesitation, he said, "If you'll permit me."

She nodded, then offered her hand. "Place two fingers here." Dr. Morgan put his middle and forefinger below the wrist. "Count the beats you feel for ten seconds. Use your brother's pocket watch. Then multiply by six—you know arithmetic, yes?"

She pulled her wrist away. "Oh, for goodness' sake, Dr. Morgan."

He seemed unfazed by the insult he'd offered. "If you can't find the pulse on the wrist or if it's too faint, try here, at the base of the neck." He touched his own neck to show her. "If his pulse is below forty, there's reason for concern."

Her father cleared his throat from the front of the car. "That's quite enough, Dr. Morgan. We must be on our way."

The trip to Penmore was quick, followed by an exchange of goodbyes. Ginger hated to leave Mrs. Martin behind. But at least here she'd be safe, wouldn't she?

Ginger leaned out of the car window to wave. The distant hoot of an owl sounded in the night, followed by the rustling of spiky branches from the tall conical evergreens beside the house. She held her breath, listening intently. The violence of the evening had left an edge on her heart. What if her mother was right? The men who'd been so angry with the Martins could come here still. Hopefully, Henry's trip to the police would deter them.

As the car pulled away down the long driveway, Ginger glanced over her shoulder at the house. The grey stone walls of the estate gleamed with moonlight.

Large, looming, safe. The home of her family and the earls of Braddock since the civil war a few hundred years earlier. Her Royalist ancestor had distinguished himself at the Battle of Braddock Down and been bestowed a title accordingly.

She couldn't help but wonder what other tribulations had befallen the gates of her home. Yet it had survived wars and plagues and conflict, hadn't it? She couldn't be the one to destroy it all with an ignorant mistake.

Taking comfort in the idea, Ginger turned back toward the car. Charlie lay on the seat in front of them, his leg in a makeshift splint. He appeared to be sleeping, thank goodness. The doctor had also appeared to have applied iodine to the cuts and scrapes on his face and arms.

Ginger's hands clenched into tight fists. Who would do this to a child? The inhumanity of it was beyond appalling. What would they have done to him if she hadn't found him?

She studied Henry's profile. "The men who did this—they did it rather brazenly. Right beside a public house. Do you think they—"

"They won't be likely to see any consequences if that is what you're asking." Henry reclined his head against the seat. His eyes were unreadable in the car's darkness.

"But they attacked you." Ginger reached toward his cheek.

He scowled and pulled back. "This world is a lot less friendly to those of our ilk than you believe, dear sister. Socialism and communism are on the rise among the lower classes. Don't be surprised if the people who resent us will take this war as an opportunity to declare their own." He dabbed at his lip with a handkerchief. "I should have asked Pierce to fetch me some ice before I left."

A chilly silence, black as the horizon, surrounded them. Henry's words had brought the fears of the evening into the car. "I don't know what my role should be in the coming months, but I can't sit back and see everything around us destroyed. If the world is changing, we must prepare to change with it. Otherwise, we'll be swept away by the winds of the coming storm."

"I don't disagree, but I can't find your place for you." Henry closed his eyes, his voice terse. "You're going to have to prove you can rise to the challenge on your own."

She stared at him in confusion as the car jolted and bumped along the road. What was Henry suggesting? She swallowed the question. If she couldn't even come up with her own way of proving her worth, then maybe Henry was right.

Poor Bosworth. A trip to London this late at night was a difficult thing to ask of him. Within a few minutes, Henry seemed to have drifted off to sleep, a skill she didn't possess. Tired as she was, she didn't sleep well outside her own bed.

Curling her knees up, she examined her ankle. The area near her ankle bone still ached when she moved her foot in a circle. Dropping back onto the seat, she covered her chest with her hand. Her heart beat was steady. Not at all what she expected.

She'd practically lit the match for Thomas Winser—or whoever had destroyed the Martins' shop and home. If she had kept her mouth shut, the Martins would have been safer.

Her throat thickened, and she wiped her eyes. Nothing had changed, despite her posturing. She'd even made things worse for herself by potentially putting herself in Stephen's favor. Stephen was the type to only give favors if he had something to gain. Tears slipped from the corners of her eyes, making trails on her cheeks.

She'd been so foolish to think she could help. After all, she possessed no skills. The only thing they meant her for was the role her father pushed her toward—to be the wife of a well-connected gentleman.

One wheel of the car hit a bump. She lurched forward. She put a steadying hand on Charlie. He moaned softly, and she switched seats, placing his head gently in her lap.

Though she was grateful Henry had agreed to come with her, she wished he would have stayed awake a while longer. Dr. Morgan had entrusted her with Charlie's care to mock her or as punishment, she was sure, but she was glad he had.

She felt helpless enough. At least now she had something to do.

Ginger closed her eyes, feeling the smooth sway of the wheels below her. Her father had been one of the first of his friends to buy a motorcar. He'd also installed a telephone well before anyone in the area. New technology fascinated him, and he kept a close eye on opportunities to invest in industry. The advantage they had now was that the new motorcar her father had purchased last year drove much faster than many others. The roads would slow them down, especially while they were still in the country.

Time seemed to pass slowly and Ginger practiced finding her own pulse. Digging her fingers into her wrist, she chewed on her lip. Nothing. She tried repositioning her fingers.

Still nothing.

Maybe she was dead.

She laughed to herself, despite it all, and tried again. Once again, she failed. *This can't be so hard, for goodness' sake.*

Frustrated at her failure to do even the most rudimentary thing, she stomped her foot. She'd conquer this. She had to practice. Reaching up to her neck, she tried there. At last, she detected the faint beating of her pulse beside her throat.

"Henry," she hissed, excitement clear in the increasing speed of her own pulse.

He groaned and opened one eye. "What?"

"Loan me your pocket watch."

"You couldn't have asked before I fell asleep?" Fumbling with his vest, he pulled it out and unclipped it. The metal was warm from his body as she took it from his outstretched hand.

She gave him an overly sweet smile, but he didn't pay attention. Within minutes, he was asleep again. Another attempt to find the pulse in her wrist proved successful, and she angled the pocket watch toward the sliver of moonlight beside her, counting it.

When she had practiced a few times, she reached for Charlie's wrist. Finding his pulse, she counted it. Strong.

Some of the tension in her shoulders relaxed.

She continued checking Charlie's pulse every fifteen minutes. Each time, she held her breath. If something truly bad happened, it would be one more thing she could add to the growing list of ways she had interfered and hurt the Martins.

When they were about twenty minutes away from London, a shriek pierced the cabin of the motorcar. Bosworth swerved upon hearing it, quickly pulling the car back onto the road.

Charlie's eyes were wide open with fright. He screamed again, rapid, panicked breaths racking his ribs.

"Charlie." Ginger shook his shoulders gently. "Charlie, calm yourself. It's all right."

The boy's eyes shut, tears finding their way from under his lids. Spittle formed on his lips and he thrashed, groaning.

"What's wrong with him?" Henry blinked blearily, sitting straighter.

"I don't know." Ginger leaned closer to him, holding him gently. "Charlie, don't move like that. You could hurt your leg. Be calm." With soft, hushing breaths, she gripped him as he sobbed and cried.

"What do we do?" Henry's brow creased with worry.

"Stay calm," Ginger ordered over Charlie's cries. "Don't add to his distress." She refocused her attentions on him, stroking his back. "Calm, Charlie. You must breathe. Deep breaths. Breathe deeply."

Then, the tautness of his body released, his sobs eased to soft hiccups. As his body became less rigid, his torso shook.

The sedative must have worn off some, or the pain intensified. His hands were tight fists, his jaw clenched.

"Mum," he managed.

"Mum will be with you as soon as she can," Ginger said, running her fingertips through his silky hair. She'd never noticed how soft a child's hair could be. Did he even remember who Ginger was right now? He seemed incoherent.

As the shadowy buildings of the city drew closer, Charlie relaxed in her arms, his cries softer. Henry scrubbed his eyes and blinked at her. "How did you do that?"

"I-I haven't the foggiest." Ginger continued to hold Charlie tight. Her response had been natural. Perhaps a maternal instinct?

Whatever it had been, she'd calmed and helped him.

She swallowed, overwhelmed, even guilty of the sense of wonder overcoming her. Helping him through the pain may have been the most satisfying thing she'd ever done.

CHAPTER SEVEN

*T*he curtain around Charlie's hospital bed parted and Ginger woke. She'd been dozing, exhausted from the long morning. Henry's pocket watch was limp in her hands. Only a few minutes before noon.

They'd driven straight to St. Thomas' Hospital in London, where Dr. James Clark had met them in the early hours before dawn. Thank goodness for inventions like the telephone. Dr. Morgan had reached his friend and apprised him of the situation hours earlier. Despite the country doctor's terrible manners, she was grateful for the favor.

Ginger stood from her chair as a nurse stepped into the small space and tidied the bed.

The nurse wore a uniform like a nun's—a long-sleeved grey dress, white apron, red cape, and a veil covering her head. How had the woman become a nurse? What had inspired her?

Being a nurse right now would be useful. Especially with the war.

Ginger's thoughts were interrupted as two orderlies brought Charlie back from surgery on a stretcher. The doctor had set the young boy's leg in a cast. His eyes were closed, his face relaxed in a deep slumber—a remarkable change from the way they'd brought him in.

The skirt of her evening gown still wore stains of his blood. Her fingertips skimmed the stiff fabric.

The curtain swayed as the doctor stepped through. James Clark was younger than Ginger had imagined a surgeon with such glowing references—he looked to be only a few years older than Henry. His dark blond hair was naturally wavy, giving him a boyish look.

Ginger approached him, clasping her handbag. "How did he do?"

"He did well. I reset the bones. He has a long road to recovery ahead of him. But I did what I could." Dr. Clark pulled off his glasses and wiped the lenses with a handkerchief. "Injuries of this nature are difficult. I can't predict how it will affect the growth of his leg."

Then Charlie might live with this forever—and not just the scars, but possibly a deformity. Her shoulders sank, her guilt heavy. "Thank you, Dr. Clark. For your help and your honesty." Most men seemed to tread carefully around her "delicate sensibilities" and leave her without a proper response to her questions.

She stepped back and nearly toppled over, pain gripping her ankle. Gasping, she reached for the first thing in her grasp—Dr. Clark's forearm.

His blue eyes were sharp. "Are you quite well?"

"I don't know." She cleared her throat and straightened, favoring the ankle which had given her trouble. "I seem to have injured my ankle last night helping the boy's mother flee from her house."

Dr. Clark raised his brows. "Flee her house?"

"It's a long story." The vicinity was filled with other patients and medical personnel, the ward rather public. She

wanted to believe the doctors and nurses here were so dedi-
cated to serving others, they wouldn't treat Charlie with the
same xenophobic fervor she'd witnessed the past few days.
But if she'd learned anything, it was to be more cautious in
what she said.

Dr. Clark offered his arm. "Perhaps you could share it
with me in the privacy of my office? It would be an excellent
opportunity for me to examine your ankle as well."

Ginger hesitated, taking a glance at Charlie. "I don't want
to leave the child by himself. My brother's gone to rest at my
aunt's house."

"I think the boy will sleep for some time."

Ginger placed her hand on Dr. Clark's arm. He was a tall,
lanky man. Though she wasn't short of stature, he made her
feel dwarfed. Her ankle throbbed, and she supported herself
on his arm as he led her through a corridor. He gave her a
shy smile as he opened a door for her. Holding it open as he
continued to hold her other arm, she had to pass under his
extended arm.

"It might be better if I support myself on the door—" she
said when Dr. Clark let go of the door. It swung closed
rapidly and hit Ginger in the forehead "—oof!"

Dr. Clark yanked the door open once more and stared at
her from the doorway, frozen in horror at what he'd done.
Then, snapping to attention, he helped her stand. "Terribly
sorry. I'm a bit clumsy, you see, and I didn't intend to knock
you over."

"I'm perfectly fine, thank you." Ginger brushed away the
impulse to feel irritated that came naturally. He'd done
nothing wrong, after all. She smoothed her skirt and gave
him a taut smile and then noticed the earnestness of his
expression, the redness of his cheeks.

She offered a more genuine smile and an attempt at

humor. "It's not every day a doctor almost injures me while trying to treat my existing injury."

It wasn't a very good joke. She cringed inwardly as his blush deepened.

"I'm so sorry, Lady Virginia—"

She'd better appear more congenial, and quickly. Though he was a stranger and she knew nothing of him, she said in a smooth tone, "Please. Call me Ginger."

He blinked, a surprised look in his eyes.

Then he knew a thing or two about how to address titled ladies properly. Her offer of friendship hadn't gone unnoticed. "Ah—is it Ginger because of the remarkable shade of hair you have?"

She smiled. "No, though it's always been a joke in my family. I'm named after my paternal grandmother—Lady Virginia Whitman, Dowager Countess of Braddock. My immediate family calls me Ginny. But on my mother's side, they always called me Ginger and my brother Henry, 'Harry.'" She stopped, feeing imbecilic. She'd yammered on about family names enough.

He fidgeted with his glasses. "I'm James. James Clark." Then he scrunched his nose. "But, you know that."

The awkward tension in the room filled the space between them again. Ginger shifted. She pointed to a chair in front of a large desk. "May I sit?"

"Oh. Of course, of course." James hurried over and held the chair for her.

Ginger eased herself into it. "Thank you."

James knelt in front of her and gestured toward her ankle. "May I?"

Ginger nodded. He tugged her long skirt up a few inches. He frowned at the stocking over her ankle. Moving his gaze back and forth between her ankles, he settled back. "From what little I can see, the left ankle appears to be swollen. Would you mind removing the stocking?"

She clasped her hands together on her lap. "May I have a moment alone?"

He exited out the door. "I'll be just outside. Please call me when you're ready. I'll leave the door open a crack so I can hear you." He turned, his back to the door, barely visible through the small slit.

The privacy allowed her some time to examine the small office. Drawn blinds obscured the light from the late morning sun. Shelves filled with bottles and books took up most of the space—not at all surprising. Very little she could use to bring up conversationally, though.

She admired him. Not only because of all the medical books with titles she didn't dare pronounce. But because he was a man who helped the hurt. With a gentleness and kindness she could only aspire to. She hadn't expected that about him either, given the behavior of the man who had referred him. Dr. Morgan could use some lessons from his friend.

She pulled up her skirt and unfastened the garter. Rolling the stocking down, she paused at her ankle and removed her shoe. She saw nothing on her ankle. "Oh really, Ginger, don't be such a ninny," she muttered to herself in a low voice.

"What's that?" James called from the doorway.

"Oh, nothing. You may come in now." Ginger neatly tucked her stocking into her shoe and set it at the base of the chair. She straightened as the door opened and then adjusted the neckline of her gown, which had shifted while she'd been leaning forward.

The doctor bent in front of her once again and examined her ankle. After asking her to turn it a few times, he sat on his heels, still holding her foot in his hands. "Well, there's no visible bruising, but it is swollen. I'd say it's just a sprain. You want to rest it, with ice." He met her gaze. "How was it this happened?"

"I was running. The Martins—" She paused. She couldn't let her experiences make her entirely cynical. And Dr. Clark had such a kind gaze. "Mr. Martin is German, you see. He's been here for ages and his wife is British-born, but now with the war, he's been imprisoned. Some radicals in the village burned the Martins' shop last night. I helped them escape."

A dark look crossed over James' face. "Say no more. I understand completely."

An apprehensive feeling gnawed at her heart. "I don't at all believe he's guilty of any crime—"

James startled, his fingers curling around the sole of her foot. "Oh, no, you misunderstand. We've seen several patients come through the last week—victims of attacks from an overzealous public. My sympathies are with Mr. Martin and his wife. What's happening is barbarous. All Englishmen should do more to make certain we aren't penalizing the innocent for the acts of others."

She smiled. At last, someone who seemed to understand her sentiments. "Yes, I quite agree." His continued hold on her foot felt strange, and she shifted. "I've been urging my father to take up the Martins' case with the Home Secretary but he's worried he'll be seen as too sympathetic to the Germans."

"McKenna and Asquith were the only ones who expressed hesitation in passing the Aliens Restriction Act." James shook his head. "Then again, Asquith has been a disappointment as the Liberal Prime Minister we hoped for."

"Well, he's certainly done little for the vote for women." Ginger checked herself. She rarely gave her political opinion publicly on the suffragette cause. Her father had made it clear he did not support his daughters becoming vocal supporters of these movements. Then again, her discomfort might be due, in part, to James continuing to hold her foot. Was this a normal part of the examination?

James' eyes were warm. "My thoughts exactly."

Ginger cleared her throat and pulled her foot back slightly.

Clearly just realizing he hadn't released her, James startled. He gave her foot a slight pat and then lowered it. "You'll be fine. I'll wrap it for you. It will help stabilize the joint. Rest and aspirin. I'll give you some."

He reached into a drawer and removed a bandage. Taking her foot once more, he wrapped it around her ankle and foot deftly. When he'd finished, he cut the bandage and tied it off. "It'll be bulky. But you'll find it hurts less because you can't bend it as easily."

He was right. She bore weight on her foot much better with the bandage on.

Ginger smiled to herself as he left her to pull her stocking on. He was an amiable man, though perhaps not the most graceful. Still, she appreciated the way he'd conversed with her. When he entered the room again, he handed her a small envelope. "Take these tablets with water. Two, every four hours. It should help the pain."

She took the envelope, clutching her handbag. "Thank you for all your help. You've been such a gift this morning." She turned to go.

"Excuse me—one thing." James grabbed a pamphlet from his desk. "You said you helped Mrs. Martin and her children flee their burning shop?"

"Yes, that's right." She didn't want to have to admit she was partially to blame for the shop's torching.

The corners of James' eyes turned up in a smile. "You're quite the heroine. May I ask—you're not married, are you?"

His boldness was astounding. Ginger's eyes widened. She

gripped her handbag tighter, hoping to keep herself from blushing. "No, no—I'm not."

James reddened. "I didn't mean—" He ran his fingers through his hair. "That's to say, while any man would be quite fortunate to have you as a wife, my interest was more professionally based." He jammed the pamphlet toward her. "The Queen Alexandra's Imperial Military Nursing Service. They have a requirement their nurses be unmarried women, you see. Given young Charlie's injuries, you clearly have a strong stomach. You might be a good match for them."

She—*a nurse?* She furrowed her brow. His echo of her unspoken thoughts, thoughts she'd barely verbalized, felt as if he'd read her mind.

She gawked at the pamphlet, then took it, hesitantly. "Nursing?" She stared at the typeface on the pamphlet. "I-I'm uncertain I'd have many skills to offer." Not to mention her father would more than likely forbid it. But still. The idea gave her a rush of excitement up her spine.

"Well, it might be something for you to consider. I am volunteering for the Royal Army Medical Corps. There will be an urgent need for doctors and nurses soon. It may be a good way for you to do your bit, if you'd like." He smiled. "St. Thomas' has a well-known program for nurses. I could put a word in for you."

He would do that? He hardly knew her. That her actions with Charlie had impressed him brought a wave of pride. Could she do something like nursing? The idea was bold. A huge departure from any role she'd ever imagined for herself. Ginger met his eyes and a strange, energetic feeling rose in her heart.

It was a laughable thought—wasn't it?

CHAPTER EIGHT

Ginger rushed into the sitting room at her aunt's house in London. She surveyed the quiet scene—Henry resting on the sofa reading the newspaper, their aunt and grandmother having tea. She kept her emotions in check and then said, "I've decided I want to be a nurse."

Her aunt, midway to lifting her teacup to her lips, paused. A curious and flabbergasted expression glimmered in her eyes. No doubt she found Ginger's appearance—still in the gown from the previous evening, hair bedraggled—to be outrageous enough. Ginger had done her best to tidy herself, but she was aware of how ridiculous she appeared for the time of day.

Henry lowered his paper and Gran turned toward her, chewing a biscuit slowly. Gran spoke first. "Heavens. It's Ginny. For a moment I thought the voices in my head were speaking aloud at last." The very faintest lilt of a Scottish accent was evident in Gran's voice. Her grandmother had been out of Scotland for most of her life, but Ginger had always loved the way she spoke.

Henry gave his grandmother a wry smile and folded his newspaper. "I highly doubt the voices in your head are declaring their desire to become a nurse." He stood and approached Ginger. Though he'd clearly slept and bathed, the bruise on his cheek still altered his appearance. "Now what's all this?"

Ginger had expected this reaction. Though they were the three people in her family who promised to be the best candidates to give the news to, she had a sudden urge to retract the statement. At least before she'd spoken it, she relished the excitement. Now she was nervous.

"She says she wants to be a nurse, you ninny." Her aunt replaced her cup on its saucer with a clink and motioned to her servant, who waited nearby to pour a third cup. "Come and have a cup of tea, Ginger dear. It's a delicious oolong. You've had a frightful night and morning. Giles can order a maid to draw a long, hot bath. And we'll fetch you some of Meg's clothes. I can hardly believe you've been wandering in public looking like that."

Ginger swallowed her disappointment. Of all people, she'd expected support from her mother's sister. Aunt Madeline was outspokenly political—a supporter of women's rights. She'd even taken Meg to some of the suffragette rallies.

"I am tired." Ginger set her handbag on the sofa. "But I'm not delusional. I want to be a nurse. At first, I thought perhaps a doctor. The London School of Medicine is just around the corner from the hospital. With the war coming, we will need women as doctors and nurses. But then I realized by the time I finish the training, the war may very well be over. So a nurse it is. I even had the matron lend me a couple uniforms so I can take them to the tailor and have some custom-made for myself."

"Nurses and doctors, my goodness, what a scandal. I can

see it now: 'Earl of Braddock's daughter to become a nurse.' Splashed all over the newspapers." Gran shuddered.

"Now, Mama, being a nurse is a perfectly respectable thing these days." Madeline stood, cup of tea in her hands, and approached Ginger. "But it's also for women who are unmarried." She held out the cup toward Ginger. "Not only is it likely you'll marry, and soon, but also you're far too beautiful to be a nurse, my darling niece. You'll have all your patients in love with you. And the wounds coming in from the battlefronts are likely to be quite gruesome."

Ginger took the cup, the sweet scent of the tea faintly reminiscent of honey. "Marriage can wait. And I'd like to do my bit. Why should the men alone be allowed to prove their love for our country?"

"Be sensible, Ginny." Henry's expression was remarkably serious. "Do you ever think Father would allow such a scheme? Is this about the Martin boy? How is he recovering?"

"He was still asleep when I left the hospital. They sedated him to keep him from the pain, but the surgery went well. And no—that's not it." She swirled the tea in the cup. "All right, partially. Charlie's injury may have inspired it. But I came up with the idea on my own. And then Dr. Clark said I had a strong stomach and suggested I look at the Queen Alexandra's."

"Doctor who?" Gran leaned toward Madeline. "You may want to dismiss Giles if we are to continue discussing this."

Madeline gave a nod to the servant. "Thank you, Giles, that will be all."

"I'm not ashamed to state I'd like to be useful to the coming war effort," Ginger said as the servant slipped out noiselessly. Being able to move without being heard must be a well-practiced art. "Dr. Clark was kind enough to take me over to speak to the matron of nurses at the college.

Normally they want entrants to be at least twenty-four, but with the war—"

"My heavens." Gran set a hand to her forehead. Ever prone to melodrama, her grandmother was acting as though Ginger had just announced her intention to become a burlesque dancer. "Who is Dr. Clark?"

Henry's eyebrows drew together with curiosity. "The surgeon we sought for the Martin boy. I didn't realize you'd become so friendly with him," he said to Ginger.

Ginger waved his comment away. "That's entirely beside the point. He examined my ankle, that's all. Which led to our conversing about the Queen Alexandra's."

"Is this Dr. Clark a handsome fellow?" Madeline asked, not bothering to hide a smirk.

"What about your ankle?" Henry crossed his arms, leaning toward her.

This wasn't going over very well. Setting her teeth together, Ginger placed the untouched cup of tea on a small table and then sat on the sofa. "He's not unattractive. Very tall. But also irrelevant."

"No—your aunt has a point." Gran came over and sat beside her. "Handsome men have a way of swaying opinions." She took Ginger's hands. "But don't let a foolish infatuation drive you to something so drastic."

Infatuation? Ginger chortled. Dr. Clark was lovely, but she wouldn't call him handsome, really. Still, he'd been too kind for her to make such a statement to her family. "I assure you, this isn't the case. I simply want to be a nur—"

"Well, it's out of the question, Ginny." Henry rubbed his jaw. "Father would never allow it."

Her grandmother's anxious expression juxtaposed with the smiling look in her aunt's eyes. A faint throb in her heart spread to a burn in Ginger's chest as she dipped her chin. "You could talk to him, Henry. Advocate for me." She scanned the room for her absent cousin. "Where's Meg when I need her? She'd be on my side."

"She went up to York with Hugh for a shoot," Madeline said. "You won't be able to marry until you're out of the service. Poor Stephen Fisher will be quite disappointed."

"Poor Stephen Fisher will have to be disappointed, regardless." Ginger reached for her abandoned tea. The adjective amused her—of all people, Stephen did little to elicit her sympathies. "I mean to refuse him."

Henry turned and walked toward one of the tall windows in the room, which overlooked the gorgeous neighborhood of Knightsbridge. He'd done his best to stay out of the whole matter. *"He's my best friend and you're my sister,"* he'd said when Stephen first proposed. *"It would be wrong of me to interfere."*

"So that's it then? You're to join the Queen Alexandra's and become a merry old maid?" Henry continued to stare out the window.

The clopping of horseshoes on the street sounded faintly from outside, followed by the honk of a horn. Every time she was in the city, the noise reminded Ginger of why she loved life at Penmore. "I don't know. I'd like to stay in at the very least while the war is on. This whole thing with the Martins has only made me understand my uselessness. I'd like to change that."

Gran placed a hand on hers. "My dear, if you'll take some advice from an old woman—you're too young to decide you'd like to spend the rest of your days alone. Now, Stephen Fisher may not be the man for you which is all right. But you're a lovely young woman. There may come a time another young man catches your fancy. If you commit to service for an organization that doesn't allow for marriage, you'll surely be setting yourself up for heartbreak when the time comes."

Madeline pursed her lips. "If it hasn't already, Mama. This Dr. Clark seems to have affected Ginger in just a morning."

Why was it her family seemed so reluctant to believe her desire to join the Queen Alexandra's could come from a need to help others? Had she given off the shallow impression her life projected? "It's entirely possible for me to have an opinion not influenced by a man, Aunt Madeline. I thought you of all people would support the idea."

Madeline laughed. "Of course, darling, but you're not me. You've always flitted about, looking for frocks, making your social calls. Also, I have the luxury of already being married and not being the daughter of an earl. Expressing one's opinion is much easier when you've already proven you're willing to sacrifice to have one."

"How utterly disappointing." Ginger narrowed her eyes at Madeline.

"Ginger, apologize to your aunt. There's no need to be rude." Gran withdrew her hand from Ginger's. "Goodness me, is this what we're coming to? A war breaks out and all manners disappear entirely?"

"She doesn't have to apologize, Mama. I wouldn't mind seeing Ginger grow more of a spine. Especially if she's as determined to join the nurses and help the German immigrants as she's declared herself to be." Madeline's eyes were a similar shade of green to Ginger's, though her hair had more of an auburn hue. Her eyes held a challenge. "Maybe Charlotte Thompson has rubbed off on you in a good way."

The mention of Charlotte was enough to get Henry's attention. "Not likely." He gave Ginger a hard look. "Don't forget you require Father's permission for all this. He holds the purse strings, after all. If you refuse Stephen, you may not humor him to allow you to join the Queen Alexandra's. Especially after all the favors you've asked for the Martins."

"If so, I'd like to see what I can accomplish for the

Martins without having to ask any further favors from father —or Stephen." Ginger pushed herself up from the sofa. As she stood, her sprained ankle erupted with pain again. She grimaced, clenching her jaw.

"What is it?" Gran reached for her arm to help her.

"I sprained my ankle helping the Martin family flee from their house last night."

Gran shook her head. "No good deed goes unpunished. Now I understand why the doctor examined you. Your aunt was too concerned with his looks to ask before."

Madeline grinned and toyed with the strand of pearls around her neck. "Oh you know, Mama, someone has to be looking for future beaus for our Ginger. Especially if she won't have Stephen Fisher."

"Ginger could have a great many beaus if she wanted them—without your help." Gran gave her daughter a pointed look.

Ginger sighed and put her teacup on the saucer. "I'm not certain that's accurate. Stephen has done his best to claim me in all our circles." Maybe Charlotte was right. She needed someone from outside their friends.

"How can he claim you when you've not accepted him?" Madeline went toward Henry. "You really must do more to discourage Stephen from scaring off other suitors, Harry. It's your responsibility as her older brother to protect her—even if it's from your own friends."

Before Henry responded, the door opened. Giles stepped through once more. "Lord Stephen Fisher is here to see Lord Henry and Lady Virginia."

"Speak of the devil and he doth appear," Gran grumbled from her place on the sofa.

Ginger smoothed her hands over the beads of her ruined dress. "I can't see him looking like this." She'd barely slept the previous night and her hair was in disarray.

"Would you like me to turn him away?" Madeline arched a brow.

"Of course not." Henry stretched, throwing an amused glance at Ginger. "Hasn't she been going on about how little she cares about what he thinks? If that's the case, what difference does it make?"

Ginger glared at Henry. "Not being interested in Stephen doesn't mean I'd love for him to see me like this."

"Well, there's hardly enough time for you to go and change now. I agree with Harry. Let him in," Madeline said to Giles. He bowed and went back out once again.

Ginger sat beside her grandmother. Gran gave her an odd look. "My dearest, you're up and down as quickly as a jack-in-the-box. Will you just settle yourself?"

Stephen came through the doorway. "Lady Westbrooke." He bowed toward Madeline, then turned toward Gran. "Lady Grey. I'm so sorry to disturb you. I heard from Lord Braddock Henry and Ginny had come to London."

"You heard from Father?" Henry asked, a hint of surprise in his features.

"Yes, he caught a train to London around noon. I'd expect he'll be here soon." Stephen removed his hat and held it in his hands. "Might I have a word alone with Henry and Ginny?"

"It just goes to show you can't buy manners," Gran said in a low whisper to Ginger. She stood and moved toward the door. "Madeline, would you call the car for me?"

Madeline followed her mother out the door.

Stephen didn't appear to have heard her, thankfully. Gran was right. The Fishers had risen to wealth only a few decades earlier, practically buying an earldom along the way. While the amount of money they had was more than enough to get them into the poshest places, it wasn't enough to buy them the credibility Ginger had often suspected Stephen desired through marrying her.

She offered him a polite smile. "Thank you for letting us know Father is on his way. Is there something the matter?"

"I've had a letter from David Peterson, my friend who is the assistant to the Home Secretary." Stephen turned his hat in his hand and then gestured toward a chair. "May I sit?"

From the Home Secretary. She held her breath. Was it possible Stephen had helped her after all? Her hope outweighed the dread of what it might mean.

"Of course." Henry came away from the window and took the seat beside Ginger. Stephen sat across from them. "I take it he has news about the Martins?"

Stephen set his hat on his knee. "Were you aware Friedrich Martin has a brother who is an *Oberst* in the Kaiser's army?"

Whatever he meant, it didn't sound good. Ginger exchanged a look with Henry. "What's an *Oberst*?" she asked.

"Colonel." Stephen folded his hands. "Both Friedrich and John Martin are on a shortlist for repatriation as a result."

If Stephen's news had been accompanied by a thunder-clap, it couldn't have been more shocking. Ginger caught her breath, feeling ill. "Repatriation? But they've done nothing wrong! They can't help who their relatives may be. What about Mrs. Martin and the other children?"

"They'll stay here. Nevertheless, the situation, especially for the elder Mr. Martin, looks grim. David said he may be able to do something for the younger Mr. Martin, but you'd both need to get to his office as soon as possible and give sworn statements in his favor. The soonest he can see you is tomorrow afternoon, though."

They would separate the family. For the length of the war? "But how can this be? The elder Mr. Martin is a kind man. Surely, we can make our appeals for him as well." Ginger's anger flared. "This is simply unacceptable."

Spots of color appeared on Stephen's cheeks. "Darling,

what more would you have me do? We've taken this to the very top. If the Home Secretary won't help, there's really no one who can."

She bristled at the term of endearment. "But we don't know the Home Secretary won't help. We know David Peterson won't help. I'm certain if we—"

Henry released an exasperated sigh. "Ginny, you're behaving irrationally. More than likely because you need to rest. While your goal is admirable, you've got to be exhausted from your long night and morning. Why not go up and rest before dinner and let Stephen and me attempt to think of alternatives? Don't forget, Stephen said there may be something he can do for John Martin. That's not nothing."

Ginger held back a sharp response. The mention of how long the day had been made her feel the exhaustion she wore in the stinging of her eyes and the dull ache in the back of her neck. The excitement she'd felt when she'd come into the room was all but extinguished. If she couldn't even manage something as straightforward as releasing an innocent man from repatriation, her other goals might be more compli- cated than she imagined.

She wasn't a suffragist revolutionary. She didn't even know if she'd consider herself a Liberal, as James had seemed to assume.

With a pang, she remembered her thoughts of the London School of Medicine for women. She'd entertained the idea with about as much strength as a deflated tire.

"Yes, and thank you, Stephen." She stood, feeling weak and tired, keeping her gaze on the gleaming oak floors and the woven rugs. "I suppose so."

Stephen and Henry got to their feet. "Perhaps you can join me for a late-night drink, Ginny? I'd love to speak to you more, darling." Stephen offered a charming smile.

I'm not your darling. She clenched her jaw. "Perhaps tomorrow?" Heaviness enclosed her heart.

She didn't want to marry him.

Even if he'd just helped her.

Now she just had to tell him no. For good.

Tomorrow.

CHAPTER NINE

Ginger limped down the staircase of her aunt and uncle's posh London home, her ankle feeling sorer than it had the day before. She paused at the bottom step, her hand resting on the curved volute of the smooth mahogany rail. The sweet scent of cakes and scones greeted her from a tray a footman carried to the parlor for elevenses. She considered popping in for a moment, but she wanted to get to the hospital.

She crossed the foyer and slipped out without announcing her intentions to Giles. Her father had mentioned going to check on Charlie late last night when he'd arrived at the house. He'd brought Violet and his valet with him also. While Ginger was thankful to have some of her own clothes and her maid to help her, she felt guilty. Her poor aunt, they were practically invading at this point. If they'd had known they needed to return to London so soon, she doubted her father would have closed the house.

Fortunately, her father had left her aunt's house again before breakfast. For all she knew, he'd already gone to visit Charlie.

Ginger hurried down the stairs and then startled as she nearly ran into a man who approached from the pavement.

Her heart squeezed in her chest. What was he doing here?

"Lady—that is, Ginger." James Clark tipped his hat. "Good morning."

"Heavens, what a surprise." Ginger gave him a broad smile as she recovered from the scare he'd given her. "I wasn't expecting to see you here."

"As it so happens, my mother has a mutual friend with your aunt. When I mentioned you to her last night, she inquired about your aunt's address for me." James returned her smile. "I wanted to call on you last night, but I thought you might be resting after all you'd been through."

"I was." She'd gone to bed early, exhausted from having spent the previous night awake. The trouble he'd gone to find her intrigued her as much as the fact that he'd mentioned her to his mother. It was charming.

Ginger checked over her shoulder, toward the house. Hopefully, neither her aunt nor Henry watched from inside.

"That's a pretty vine." James pointed to her aunt's garden, where a carefully cultivated vine with purple flowers grew toward the window.

"Clematis, I believe." Ginger motioned toward the pavement. "Shall we? I was just headed toward the hospital."

James fell into step beside her. "How is your ankle this morning?"

"Better." *Now why had she said that?* It hurt worse than ever. She didn't want to trouble him with it, though. "I'll be just fine. How's Charlie? I'm eager to see him."

James's face grew more serious. "Charlie has a fever, I'm afraid. Hopefully nothing serious, but it could be a sign of infection. He'd just fallen to sleep after a long night awake when I left the hospital." He cleared his throat. "But we can go back to the hospital together."

Ginger's fingers tightened on her handbag. Much as she wanted to say yes, London wasn't one of those towns she could wander about without being spotted by someone she knew. If someone saw her with James, it might get back to Stephen and...

She frowned. Why was she behaving as though Stephen had the right to dictate if she go to the hospital with James? Stephen didn't own her. And though he may have proposed, she had every intention of telling him no. A warm breeze enveloped her and the white clouds drifting overhead didn't indicate rain. She might have brought a parasol. She'd spent the summer trying to avoid the freckles that came so naturally to her skin.

The scent of petrol from a passing car wafted across the pavement. She turned, examining James' profile. He was a nice-looking man, though not particularly what she would call handsome. And she'd enjoyed their brief conversations. "I'd be delighted."

The smile James gave her made it clear how pleased he was she'd accepted. "I'm glad. I was at luncheon with my mother at Hotel Cecil and it seemed a waste to be so close to where you were without checking. We can walk back that way if you'd like. I'd love for you to meet her. She was fascinated by what I told her about how you handled Charlie."

"Hotel Cecil?" Ginger gave him another look. For a doctor, he certainly seemed to have connections with the upper class. She'd attended a few functions at Hotel Cecil over the Season. She'd have to make a note to inquire about him further. "The distance to the Strand may be more of a walk than my ankle can handle."

He led her toward an open-topped car parked a block away from her aunt's house. "How silly of me. I'll drive you. It'll only be a quick visit. I can take you back to the hospital afterward so you can complete your mission to visit the Martins."

"My, you drive your own car as well? Then you have more skills than a surgeon's." Ginger slid into the passenger seat as he held the door for her, the leather of the seat warm against her thighs through her skirt. Was she flirting? She didn't want him to get the wrong impression of her.

James climbed in and started the car. "You'll find me to be a man of many talents." He laughed and pulled away from the curb. "Did you give any more thought to the QA program?"

"I'd love to be a nurse. The more I consider it, I'd like to have some useful skills to offer. Do something that really matters for the war effort." Her throat hurt from speaking loudly to be heard over the thrumming of the engine.

James gave her a warm look. "I'm pleased to hear it."

She settled into the seat, enjoying the feeling of the sun on her skin, and the rush of the wind as they drove. London seemed to be turning into a recruitment center for the army —a result of the olive and tan uniforms worn by new soldiers on the streets. Buildings were papered with recruitment posters.

The feeling of excitement she'd felt about nursing came rushing back to her. The wind whipped a feathery strand of hair into her eyes and she pushed it off her face. Being in the car with James, heading to Hotel Cecil with no one in her family even knowing where she was—it was exhilarating.

More than that. She felt bold and capable. In control of her own affairs. And the company was enjoyable, too. James was more interesting by the minute.

She carried the feeling of boldness with her after she parted from James and visited Charlie. As the boy was still resting, the nurse on duty turned her away, much to Ginger's frustration. Ginger didn't want Charlie to awaken and find himself alone. Though she didn't know the boy well, she couldn't help but feel a bond with him, given what they'd been through together.

Still, the hospital gave her an unusual sense of direction. She waited outside the ward until she finally had a few minutes to see him and then headed back to her aunt's house. As she arrived, Henry came rushing out of the sitting room toward her.

"Where on earth have you been?" Henry's heels struck against the polished floor with an echo.

"I popped by Hotel Cecil and then stopped in at the hospital to visit Charlie." She removed her hat. "Where's Father? I'd hoped to see him there." She'd prepared herself on the trip back from the hospital to tell her father about her intention to be a nurse. She didn't want time and fear to build up and prevent her making her announcement.

Henry peered at her. "Alone?"

"Actually, no. James Clark came by to check on me as I left to go to the hospital. I went with him. He wanted to introduce me to his mother—a lovely lady." Her aunt's remarks the day before would make it more of an issue to Henry than it really was. She liked James, but he wasn't what she would consider as a potential beau. She barely knew him.

Henry frowned. "Madeline may have been right in questioning your interest in Dr. Clark."

Embarrassment pricked at her chest. "Honestly, Henry. If I were interested in him, I would be more than willing to tell you about it." Not that she'd even known the man long enough to entertain such thoughts. Then again, James had introduced her to his mother. She might have thought about what it would mean to him before she'd agreed to it.

"Yes, well—" Henry tapped his pocket watch. "The fact is, your visit with him has made us late to meet with David Peterson. Given your interest in the Martin case, I'm shocked you've lost track of time so profoundly."

Oh no. She'd have fly-aways in her hair from the car trip with James and there wouldn't be time to change. How could she have forgotten?

She'd been busy asking James what she needed to do to prepare for nursing training. Her mind had buzzed with ideas. Something about the whole idea—sitting at the bedside of injured soldiers, holding their hands, soothing their worries—sounded so marvelously useful that she'd become distracted.

"Do I look completely disheveled?" She hastened to a mirror.

Henry grabbed her by the elbow and steered her toward the door. "You'll look more disheveled when you're flustered because we missed our appointment." He led her outside.

"Easy now. My ankle is still hurting. Is Stephen going to meet us there?" Madeline's chauffer waited just beyond the steps beside the car. Ginger accepted his help into her seat. The interior of the motorcar smelt of warm, polished leather. Henry sat beside her.

"Stephen won't be there." Henry paused as the door shut behind them and lowered his voice. "I would exercise caution with how loudly we discuss the matter in front of others." He gave a nod toward the chauffer as he climbed into the driver's seat.

"I'm feeling like a prisoner in my own country, just for expressing an unpopular opinion," Ginger muttered.

"Ironic, when your chief complaint is about men who have actually been imprisoned." Henry chuckled and nudged her side. "Father worries you're growing alarmingly political, little sister."

Her father would be worried about such a notion. She gave him a wry smile. "We wouldn't like that, would we?"

"All I'll say is you ought to be careful. Our lot is not the same as Dr. Clark's, for example, regardless of his father's knighthood and his mother's wealth."

Her jaw dropped. She didn't know whether to be furious or find him endearing. "You looked him up?" Now it was Ginger's turn to laugh. Of course, Henry had. She hadn't given too much thought to her aunt's claims the day before, but Henry would have. He'd always been protective of her.

His findings about James were intriguing, though. The good doctor apparently had more to recommend him than she'd first imagined. He could easily make a match with any girl from a proper family. No father could object to that background—including hers.

"Given your interest in him, I felt obliged to." Henry didn't look the least apologetic.

She shifted in her seat, adjusting her gloves so that they dug into the spaces between her fingers less. "Well, as much as I appreciate the research you've done into his background, there's nothing to be concerned about. And I know my place —or at least the one defined for me. But I won't sit about during this war and do nothing to help. The life I've lived has been comfortable, but it's also been a handicap, Henry. I don't know how to do anything."

Henry's green eyes were thoughtful, as though he was seriously considering her statement. "But will being a nurse truly make you happy? The labor is something you're wholly unaccustomed to."

"I think so, yes." At least he didn't seem to rule out the idea with the same lack of consideration he'd displayed the day before.

"I'm not certain Father will agree." Henry leaned forward, his face relaxing in the breeze coming from the window. "This is perfect hunting weather, by the way. It's a pity I missed what will likely be the last shoot of the year."

Ginger reached over and touched his arm. "Tell me it

doesn't make you feel more worthwhile to be helping the Martins than out there on a silly shoot." A loud motorcar roared by, filling the air with fumes. She focused on the ugly bruise on her brother's face. "I'm proud of you. You were quite heroic."

Henry gave her a light-tipped smile. "Heroic is a generous word, but thank you." His gaze drifted out the window once again. "I only hope someday to be worthy of the favorable opinion you have of me, Ginny. I'm not as good as you. The world appears uglier to my more cynical mind, I suppose, and I know the part I must play in it."

Something about his words seemed ominous. "Don't be ridiculous. You're a good person. Better than I am. I always seem to be the one getting into trouble."

The somber tension that had crept into their conversation eased as Henry snorted. "Well, I suppose that's true. I only wish I could take credit for all those tricks you played on our governesses."

Despite diverting from the more serious conversation to reminisce about their childhood, the conversation they indulged in for the rest of the drive was soothing to the heaviness on Ginger's heart. By the time they reached David Peterson's office, Ginger felt more herself than she'd felt for days. Henry had always had a knack for that.

David ushered them into his office, his brown shoes squeaking as he walked. He was rather a dandy—Ginger was convinced his coat alone was more expensive than her own outfit. He'd carefully slicked back his groomed dark hair with pomade. In his hand, he held a fine cigar and quickly offered one to Henry by displaying a case.

Ginger's eyes drifted over the pictures on his desk, a few of him with what appeared to be foreign dignitaries and one on safari in Africa, where he stood beside a prized kill. She averted her gaze as he sat at his desk and invited them to sit in the two chairs across from him.

"I can't tell you how pleased I am to meet you," David said to Ginger. "Stephen tells me you are to be married soon."

Has he really? Ginger fumed, arranging her handbag on her lap with delicate care as she restrained her anger. "It's not quite settled."

David gave her a blank, confused, blinking expression.

Would he be less apt to help her if he didn't believe her to be Stephen's fiancée? She gritted her teeth and then tried, more amicably, "Well, with the war, it's not the best time to plan a wedding."

"Ah, quite right." David nodded and tapped his cigar, the ash swirling into a crystal tray on his desk. "I see." He turned his gaze to Henry. "So as I understand it, you'd like to sign a statement to support a—" his eyes scanned a paper in front of him "—John Martin. To keep him from repatriation."

"Actually, Mr. Peterson," Ginger cut in, "I wanted to discuss the possibility of preventing the repatriation of both John and his father, Friedrich Martin. We've known them for years."

David frowned. "I'm afraid that's quite impossible. Mr. Martin has a—"

"Yes, Stephen informed us of the situation." Ginger leaned forward eagerly. "But, Mr. Peterson, you must see it would be wrong of us to make assumptions about Mr. Martin based on his brother."

"I don't see that, Lady Virginia, and neither should you." The friendly tone with which David had addressed her earlier grew frosty. The corners of his eyes narrowed. "We can't put the comfort of one man above the safety of our country, and there's no reason to believe he's not a risk."

His curt tone made her feel insignificant. The man might

have a point, but she wouldn't concede it. Not when he'd been so rude about it.

Henry, who could always be far suaver than she was in these situations, gave David a smooth smile. "Mr. Peterson—you mistake my sister's zeal for this situation for a lack of patriotism. My sister knows Friedrich Martin's wife quite well—" a lie, but Henry could pull it off effortlessly "—and given their close relationship, she's had no reason to question Mr. Martin's loyalty to the Crown. But I assure you, she's as devoted to the cause as one can be."

Ginger wanted nothing more than to be quickly done with this meeting, her face flushing. "Yes, in fact. I've just come from St. Thomas' Hospital. I'm planning on joining the Queen Alexandra's Imperial Nursing Service."

David looked from Henry to Ginger, as though trying to decide what to make of them. Then his posture shifted, his shoulders relaxing. "That's wonderful." He removed some papers from a file in front of him. "As I was saying, John Martin has a few things recommending him to be simply kept in internment during this conflict. I'll need you both to sign these statements I've prepared for you." He set the papers down in front of them.

Henry lifted the papers and scanned them.

Ginger's gaze drifted back to the safari picture. "Did you know, Mr. Peterson, Stephen recently bought an estate in Cape Town?" She was glad she'd paid polite attention while Stephen had droned on about it over the summer at one event they'd attended together. It lent her the advantage of being certain David Peterson didn't know about the Cape Town estate. Stephen had reiterated throughout the conversation several times about how the estate would be for his exclusive use, far from the reach of the many friends who hung about him *"like gnats, waiting for fruit to drop."*

Given his clothes and his pompous attitude, she wouldn't be surprised if David Peterson was one such friend.

David gave her a faltering glance.

Yes, exactly, you silly little man.

She settled back in her seat, crossing her feet by her ankles. "He's quite excited about it. And he's very keen to invite some close friends after the war." She avoided Henry's watchful gaze, knowing he'd be aware of what she was up to. The thought threatened her poise for the briefest moment. "Given your willingness to help me in this matter, I'll be sure to tell Stephen you're to be the first to see it."

Just as she prepared to ask about Mr. Martin again, Henry handed her the papers. "What are the chances of speeding along John Martin's naturalization? His siblings and residency make him an excellent candidate. He's lived in our village all his life, save for three months after his birth." Henry handed Ginger a pen.

Ginger gritted her teeth, her frustration with Henry growing. She'd been so close to her goal of pressing David again about Mr. Martin—why on earth had Henry stolen her opportunity and refocused the conversation on John again? She scrawled her elegant signature on the space beside Henry's.

David pursed his lips and flipped through the file in front of him. His eyebrows drew together. Glancing up, his gaze landed on Ginger first, before going back to Henry. "It certainly seems like a good possibility. But I'd have to hurry. And ask for some favors. He may be required to sign up for service."

"Excellent." Henry stood. "I'll come back to inquire about the matter tomorrow."

Ginger understood Henry's cue to leave and got to her feet.

David placed his hands on the desk and leaned against the top. He addressed Henry. "And will you be signing up?"

"I'll be joining my father at the Foreign Office in Cairo," Henry said. "We leave the week after next, which is part of our urgency with the Martin matter."

"Cairo?" David broke into a smile. "I have a friend who's just recently returned from there. I should make an introduction. The man is an absolute genius of a linguist. He might give you some wonderful insights into the political climate there now."

"I'd be in your debt." Whether Henry had any intention of contacting David's friend wasn't clear, but he did a good job of making even Ginger think he was truly interested.

David leaned down and scribbled on the back of a card. He handed it to Henry. "Mr. Noah Benson. I'll send him a note." He lifted his chin toward Ginger. "Don't take your sister with you to meet him. Half of the ladies I know are in love with him—including my sister."

Ginger laughed. "With such a recommendation, I'm sure I'd be happy to stay away. Men surrounded by admirers are boorish." She was also certain any man who was a friend of David Peterson would likely be a man she'd want to steer clear of.

She put her hand on Henry's elbow. "We should leave, Mr. Peterson, but thank you so much for your help."

As they made their way onto the street, Ginger allowed herself to seethe at Henry. "Why did you stop me from asking about Friedrich Martin—he's going to be sent away."

"You were overplaying your hand, Ginny. It was a good attempt and I think it will motivate Mr. Peterson to help with something realistic. Like John's naturalization. But Friedrich is beyond our help. You must accept that."

"Well, I don't accept it." Ginger glared at Henry and scanned the street for the car. Still, if John naturalized, it would mean he wouldn't be interned at all. Having her son back would be a relief to Mrs. Martin—and a help. "You took advantage of the suggestion I made and took a gamble."

Henry's lips curled into a smile. "Precisely. And if it works, I'll give you full credit." He held out his arm for her as they stepped into the road. "Though David Peterson won't be too happy to learn you're doing your very best to turn Stephen down."

Ginger dodged around a motorcar honking at them as they crossed the street. "David Peterson doesn't need to know." She batted her lashes at him. "For now."

"Poor devils. I'm practically complicit in your treachery, Ginny." Henry rubbed his jaw.

"Always. I wouldn't have it any other way." Her laughter belled behind them, and they hurried toward the car.

CHAPTER TEN

"Considering that I've been here for a full day, trying to catch an appointment with you is nearly as difficult as getting an audience with the king," Ginger's father complained as he sat down beside her.

They'd gone through to the sitting room after dinner with Madeline and Henry—both of whom had excused themselves for early bedtimes.

Ginger rotated the stem of her glass of cream sherry, the light from the chandelier winking off the crystal. "I haven't been avoiding you. I had hoped to see you at the hospital earlier. I just feel terrible for poor Charlie Martin, lying all alone in a city far from home."

"You have a kind heart, Virginia. But if we remain here much longer, it would be wrong of us to take advantage of your aunt's hospitality. And opening the home in London is illogical, considering we're about to leave the country." Her father settled back in his seat, against a round golden pillow in the settee's corner. "It's time for us to go home. We have given the boy world-class care. You've advocated as much as you can for the Martin men. We have other issues to attend to now."

Her heart fell. He must have heard about her plans to enter the nursing service. This was his subtle way of building an opposition.

Ginger glanced at her father. Despite the difference in their gender, she was nearly as tall as he was, a fact that had slowly shifted something about the way she saw him. When she was a child, he'd seemed so large and looming. Capable and powerful. He still smelled the same—a mix of tobacco and cedarwood. In her girlhood, she'd stolen one of his embroidered handkerchiefs to keep it nearby when she slept, soothed by it.

She preferred to be direct about the matter. "You've heard then? That I want to join the Queen Alexandra's?"

His mouth set in a line under his trim mustache. "Yes, I've heard. I thought to give you the courtesy of telling me yourself."

"But not before you formed an opinion against it." Ginger finished the remaining sherry in her glass. She was glad they were alone. This wasn't a conversation she wished to have in front of her aunt. Or Henry. The glass in her hand felt like an obstacle she wished to be rid of.

"I'm not interested in marrying Stephen Fisher." She stood and crossed the room, setting the glass on a small tray. Keeping her back to her father briefly, she summoned her strength. She had to convince him. "I don't love him. The truth is, I'm not sure I could ever love him. And—I want to do something more with myself. Just being in the hospital the last few days has been invigorating."

She turned and met his gaze with a strong lift to her chin. "I want to be useful to my country. I want to feel as though I have a skill that makes me worthy of being on this earth.

Something more than being able to smile politely and hang on the arm of my future spouse as a prize he's won."

"Oh, for goodness' sake." Her father stood with a shake of his head. "This is not what I sent you into London for. Training as a nurse is out of the question."

"And why not? I went to Hotel Cecil today and ran into Lady Forsythe and she mentioned her niece is signing up—"

"The Forsythes are not our family." Her father paced in front of the empty fireplace and then scratched his temple. "And frankly, I don't care what they or any other family in the whole of England do. You will not be joining such a disgusting profession. You don't know what you're asking. War is something you've never truly experienced. You may think it's glorious and adventurous now—but two weeks in the middle of war and you'll be begging for Penmore and the comforts you take for granted."

Did she really give the impression of being so soft and spoiled? She recoiled at his glare, frustration clawing at her belly. "I'm not as weak as you seem to think. I believe I can handle a great deal more, in fact."

"Perhaps. But you won't be handling the wounded men of England. Now, I've had enough of this delay with Stephen. An alliance with him will help secure our family's future."

"Yes, but why me with him? If what you seek is to join our family to the Knotley fortune, then look to Henry. He's already more than in love with Angelica."

Her father gave a guttural sigh of frustration. "And look what happened with Charlotte Thompson. Angelica is young and barely knows her own mind. Not to mention Henry isn't the only young man chasing after her. We should cement what's certain—Stephen's offer to you."

Much as Charlotte had always been a close friend and ally, Ginger hated that her friend's happiness in marrying the man she wanted had put her in this position. "Well, I won't have him. I'm joining the QAs. And there isn't anything you can do to change my mind."

Her father's face reddened, his fingers curling into his palms. "How dare you be so selfish? You won't be speaking so boldly when you find yourself cut off financially."

Her breath caught. "You would really cut me off for joining the nursing service?"

"Yes. And more. I did some digging after your brother told me what you were considering. The Queen Alexandra's rarely accept women under the age of twenty-four. You're too young. I won't give my consent."

She set her hands on her hips. "I don't need your consent. I'll get permission." James had suggested he could help her bypass the stipulation, regardless. "And I'll learn to survive without the money."

"If you think my influence won't determine your acceptance into the nursing program, you've been deluding yourself," her father snapped. He went up to the fireplace and set one hand on the mantel, leaning his weight forward.

Her lips parted with shock. He'd never been this aggressive with her. "You wouldn't dare do that."

"Wouldn't I? I don't approve of your joining it. I don't want my daughter joining an organization which makes old maids out of their applicants." Her father stared stonily into the empty hearth before turning toward her, an appeal on his face. "But I may compromise. If you settle your engagement, then I will give you my blessing. You can spend your time in the nursing service and then marry Stephen as soon as the war ends."

His manipulation appalled her. The floorboards creaked as she inched closer to him, fighting back tears. "You would have me marry a man who will never make me happy to make your fortunes feel more secure. That's it then? I'm simply a pawn to be traded in marriage. And if I don't consent, you'll make it impossible for me to do anything I truly desire."

Her father's face softened. "I want you to be happy. I do. But you're being short-sighted with all of this. Happiness is a choice."

Ginger clasped her hands in front of her. "I'm disappointed in you, Father. First your tepid support of the Martins, now this. But perhaps I gave you too much credit for being fair."

Inhaling sharply through his nose, her father straightened, his shoulders falling back. "I've seen war before, Virginia. In South Africa, during the Boer War. I saw the camps holding the Afrikaners when we interned them—women and children—in a terrible state. War is horrific. You are inexperienced. You've never wanted for hunger or lived in discomfort—and I'm proud of it. Accuse me of selfishness if you must, but I have always striven to give my family the best this world offers, and I'm not ashamed of it."

"But then how can you simply wash your hands of the Martins? Right there—having seen internments before—should be evidence enough that it can be wrong, Father. Not all the Germans living in England are spies. This is the stuff of those Oppenheim novels from your library—not real life."

"It is reality!" Her father's voice thundered and he visibly ground his teeth before continuing. "There are spies among us. Also, fear is an incredibly powerful motivator. The fear of the public, the fear of one's enemy, the fear of loss—all of it in time of war has the potential to act as a powder keg ignited with the vagaries of human emotion."

"And therefore, there is to be no justice? Fear must win? I don't—" she gathered her thoughts, her head spinning with a jumble of emotions "—I won't accept that. I will not simply stand by and watch justice be held hostage to the court of public opinion. No more so than I will back away from becoming a nurse."

Her father's eyes sliced at her with fury. "Then you will promise to marry. Or you will find doors closed in front of you faster than you can even speak your name. We leave for Penmore tomorrow."

Ginger's cheeks flamed as he strode from the room. Her knees wobbled, the elegant room wavy through her eyes. She'd expected him to be angry, but to threaten to disown her and cut her off? Surely her mother would never allow it.

Then again, what choice did her mother have? The world didn't look kindly on women—her mother didn't control her father any more than she controlled the family's finances.

Tears pricked her eyes. What was she going to do?

CHAPTER ELEVEN

*C*harlie Martin's face was peaceful as he slept. Ginger stood at the foot of his bed, hesitant to wake him. She didn't want to leave town without telling him goodbye. The thought of not being here to help him made her furious with her father all over again. With Mrs. Martin forbidden to travel, who would look after him?

Madeline might help. Her aunt had a good heart. Ginger would have to discuss it with her when she returned. She'd slipped out of the house before dawn, unwilling to have her father pull her away before she'd visited Charlie one last time.

He startled just then, his arms shifting before his eyes fluttered open, heavy with sleep. His eyes crossed the space, his expression unchanging and, for a moment, Ginger thought he'd drift back to sleep. But his eyes landed on her. He closed them again. "Is my mum here?" he mumbled in a low voice.

Ginger came closer. "No, Charlie. Remember what I told you yesterday afternoon? Your mother can't come to London."

He didn't open his eyes, but he nodded. "I need my legs to work. To help her."

Her heart broke for him. The responsibility on his shoulders must feel so heavy, and he was just a child. If only her family weren't leaving for Egypt—Ginger could have begged her father to take on one of the older girls as a kitchen maid. But as it was, they were closing the house which meant no additions to their large staff.

She set a hand on his shoulder. "Charlie, I must leave today. For Penmore. I can't promise when I'll be back, but I'll give your mother news of you. Is there anything you want me to tell her?"

Charlie opened his eyes. The blueness of his irises was striking, his eyes shiny. "Tell her I'll do what the doctor says so I can come home soon and help her. And I miss her."

Ginger nodded, a lump rising in her throat. "I will tell her."

"Oh—and my little sister Millie..."

"Yes?"

"She's afraid of the dark. Might be more afraid now. Tell her to think about the magical garden. It helps."

His devotion to his family was so touching and resilient. Ginger wanted to carry him off, back home, where he could convalesce near them and be given the peace of mind that all would be well. But James had said it would be at least a few more weeks before he could leave the hospital.

As she left him, she noticed James at the doorway to the ward. He hung back, but appeared to have been watching her. She approached him and gave him a tight smile. A sharp breath brought with it the scent of alcohol and antiseptic and she wrinkled her nose. "I've just come to take my leave. I'm to travel back to Somerset today."

"I take it your father didn't give you his blessing to join the nursing service?"

She looked away from him, not wanting him to see the tears threatening her vision. She'd cried well into the night. "No, he's afraid I'll waste my life as an old maid. He wants to see me settled, at least with an engagement, before I make the commitment to train. It gives him some level of security to think that when the war ends, I'll marry rather than stay a nurse."

"He loves you. No father wants to see his beautiful daughter grow old without the comfort of a husband." James seemed to realize a moment too late he'd called her beautiful and he looked at the ward, his face reddening further as he rubbed the back of his neck. "Can I walk you outside?"

Ginger nodded. He thought she was beautiful. He really was an amiable man. Too bad she didn't have any interest in him. He would have made a much nicer prospect than Stephen Fisher. "That would be lovely."

They started out of the ward and James fell into step beside her, despite his longer stride. "When will you sign up for the Medical Corps?" Ginger asked him.

"Actually," James cleared his throat, "I signed up yesterday. I must get fitted for a uniform this week."

"Oh, that's wonderful." Ginger smiled. She was genuinely glad for him—if not a little jealous. "That reminds me—I must give back those nursing uniforms you arranged for me to borrow." How foolish she'd been, borrowing uniforms to have her own tailor-made. She hadn't thought her father would make it so impossible for her to join. "I'll send them over with one of my aunt's servants."

"Whenever you have the chance." James' posture bent, as though he was accustomed to trying to make himself smaller for private conversations. "Are you certain your father won't reconsider?"

"I don't think he will." Her throat tightened, frustration bubbling too close to her heart. The wound was still too fresh for her to dwell on it here, though. She gave him as bright a smile as she could muster. "I'm certain you'll do us all proud, Dr. Clark."

"Well," the corners of his eyes crinkled. "I don't know what wartime surgery will be like, but I hope I can be useful to our Tommies. With the first wounded already arriving, the time has come for me to get over there, where I can have a greater impact right away."

His sense of duty and bravery were commendable. "Then you'll go to the front lines?"

"That's my wish."

How wonderful it must be to act as one wished. Her resentfulness marred her ability to be fair right now. Their steps echoed as they entered a stairwell and made their way down. Despite only having known him for a few days, James felt more like a confidant than even some of her closest friends—if only because she could talk about something like nursing training with him. He didn't find the idea scandalous or strange.

"Perhaps as the war goes on, my father will relent and allow me to train to be a nurse. It may be easier once he sees the need." The heaviness of her heart told her it was also a wistful dream. Her father wouldn't be likely to be persuaded if she disregarded his wishes and didn't agree to marry.

"And your father really insists you must be engaged beforehand?" James adjusted his glasses as they stepped out into the bright August morning.

"Yes." She shook her head with a chortle. "But getting engaged with the stipulation I'll wait until the war is over to marry may be a great deal to ask of a man." She doubted Stephen would find that acceptable. Something had even tempted her to tell him yes, just to get what she wanted—and break it off with him later. But it would just be deferring the problem. Her father wasn't likely to react kindly to being deceived.

Unless Stephen happened to die in battle, which even she couldn't think of as a solution. *What a horrid thought, Ginger.*

"I suppose it depends on the man. Some might be willing to wait." They reached the edge of the pavement and Ginger stopped. James flagged a taxi cab approaching them and it stopped a few feet away.

Ginger grinned and a breeze ribboned past, scattering a few leaves from the trees near the entrance to the hospital. "Thank you for all your help, Dr. Clark." Holding out her hand, she offered it to him. "And thank you for all your help with Charlie. Godspeed to you in the army. I'll keep you in my prayers."

He bowed and then kissed the back of her hand. "Please do call on me for anything. I don't know how much longer I'll be at St. Thomas' but I'm happy to help while I can."

Ginger left him and made her way to the car. By the time she'd settled in her seat, he'd gone back into the hospital. With a pang of her heart, she sighed deeply stared forward as the car drove away. Leaving Charlie in the hospital didn't feel right to her, but she was glad James could still see to his care.

The trip to Madeline's house was short, but it gave enough time for her to find the composure to face her father. She was disappointed with his lack of support for her ideas, but more than anything, he'd hurt her. When Stephen had proposed and her father had made it clear he wished for her to accept, she'd still felt he would respect her choice. Now it was clear he meant to punish her if she didn't do what he wanted. Had she missed the signs of his control before? She'd always thought him to be more reasonable and interested in her happiness before now.

As the car slowed, the verdant trees and grasses threw a yellowish green hue into the windows from Hyde Park. She inhaled the familiar scents of city life—the mixture of smoke and petrol with food and warm summer air, tinged with sweat. When would she next be able to appreciate a London summer?

She paid the driver and stepped out of the car, feeling lost and yearning for...something. The feeling of purpose, she decided, as she stared at the couples strolling down the pavements. Young men in their army uniforms, their wives or sweethearts at their sides. Across the country, it seemed the olive uniforms popped up more and more each day.

She didn't want to belong to the war—a garish thought. But to the mission of serving others, of putting her own life to the side.

The stone balustrade was cool to her touch as she ascended the steps to her aunt's house. Violet had come out with her father and his valet a few days earlier—hopefully she would have packed Ginger's things. Now that she was going, Ginger didn't want to delay any longer than necessary.

Giles opened the door for her, and she thanked him, hurrying through to the foyer as she slipped off her gloves.

"My lady, Lord Stephen Fisher is here to see you. He's in the library with your brother now," Giles informed her.

Ginger halted in mid-step and caught her balance on a console table. Embarrassed by her lack of grace, she stiffened and gave Giles a sheepish smile. "Ah, well, in that case—lead the way."

Had her father said something to him? His appearance here so early seemed more than well-timed. What if her father had told him she meant to refuse him?

She hadn't prepared herself mentally to see Stephen this morning. Her argument with her father from the night before wasn't sufficiently behind her to not feel her resentment toward Stephen unfurl in the flare of her nostrils and snake its way up her gut. She wasn't in the mood to entertain him. Or pretend she had any desire to consider seriously marrying him. No matter how much he'd helped with the Martins.

Her anger subsided when she saw Henry first. He and Stephen were in the middle of an animated conversation. Henry's infectious laughter filled the space. She had to be reasonable. *Careful.* If not for herself, then for the sake of Henry's relationship with Stephen—and Angelica.

The two men composed themselves when they saw her. Stephen flashed her a dazzling smile. "Ginny, darling. How lovely you look this morning."

His term of endearment made the hair on the back of her neck stand on end. *Not today.* Today she couldn't take it.

Ginger smoothed her hands on her walking skirt. She had dressed for travel, not for company. Still, Stephen had always been quick to compliment her. "I'm surprised to see you here." Ginger approached them and folded her hands. "It's so early."

Henry and Stephen exchanged a look. "Shall I tell her?" Stephen smiled more broadly this time and came forward, taking her hands. "I've just had news from David Peterson— first thing this morning. He's arranged the naturalization for John Martin, and it looks as though we may stop the repatriation of Friedrich Martin for now. He's being kept in internment, but not sent to Germany."

What?

Ginger's jaw opened, her anger and resentment dissolving.

The news she'd hoped for. *Everything* she'd been working for.

Despite Stephen being the one to deliver the news, its impact was not lost.

"How wonderful!" Ginger laughed as Stephen caught her

in an embrace. Even that didn't bother her for the moment. John was going to be free.

Stephen pulled back, but kept his hands on her shoulders. "Well, when David told me last night about how you'd told him about inviting him to the Cape Town estate, I had my father pull a few strings with Secretary McKenna." The gleam of excitement in Stephen's eyes was infectious.

But—oh.

Oh no.

Stephen believed she intended to accept his offer.

Henry must have seen the panic on her face—he cleared his throat. "I'll leave you two to speak for a few minutes. Madeline had some questions for me about a new motorcar she's considering buying."

In the fading echo of Henry's footsteps, Ginger felt her face burn, her heart racing. What was she to say?

She'd overplayed her hand. *Blasted David Peterson.*

Stephen held her hands and pulled her closer. "Darling, is this what I've longed for? You've finally accepted my offer of marriage?" His lips focused on hers, the space between them closing fast.

She dodged his kiss and twisted out of his arms. "No," she choked out, her throat acidic. "No, I'm sorry, Stephen, but no." Tears stung at her eyes. "I can't marry you."

He stiffened and gave her an odd look, his gaze clouding. "Whatever do you mean?"

"I mean—I admire what you've been able to do for the Martins. And I appreciate your friendship with Henry, but I don't love you. I can't marry you just because of those things. It's not enough for me."

Stephen's face grew pale as his ears turned pink. "You're refusing me? But why?"

Why, indeed, when he could give her every comfort?

Except love. Love wasn't supposed to make her shiver with repulsion, and yet his gazes did precisely that.

"I just don't—"

Stephen held out a hand. "You don't need to say it again. You've already wounded me enough." His eyes narrowed. "Then you were just using my influence to get your way, was that it? And I'm the heartless one." He huffed, a choked, angry growl in his throat.

"I never meant to manipulate you."

"No, you just wanted to manipulate David Peterson." He shook his head in disgust. "And here I rejoiced in his words. Because I never would have imagined you to be anything other than genuine."

Ginger lowered her gaze, chastened. "I didn't mean for it to get back to you."

"Well, at least you're being honest now." Stephen paced for a moment and shook his head.

Speaking of which.

"Wait—" The circumstances were the worst possible to bring up the subject, but she had no choice. "What did Mr. Peterson say about John Martin? What do we have to do for the naturalization?"

The look Stephen shot her was icy. For a flash, Ginger thought he might not respond. Then he said in a stiff tone, "He has an appointment in five days at the office of the Home Secretary. He'll need paperwork to be transported from the internment camp and then he'll have to sign the Oath of Allegiance. David said he would telephone Henry to make the arrangements."

Ginger swallowed, her throat dry. She was a terrible person for taking advantage of him like this. "Stephen, I'm truly sorry. I didn't mean to hurt you."

The corners of his mouth turned down. "You'll change your mind. We were meant for each other."

She squared her shoulders, even though she didn't feel strong now. She felt awful. Like a manipulative, cruel woman. "No, I don't think so. But maybe when my family returns from Egypt, we can be friends."

He gave a scoffing laugh. "As though that would ever be enough to satisfy me." He loosened his collar. "I was going to tell you another time, but I'm going to Egypt to work with your father. And my father is going to allow Angelica to come with me—she's very keen to see Egypt and with Henry going, she wanted to be close to your family."

She didn't know whether to feel sorry for him or to be dismayed he was following her family to Egypt.

He spread his hands in front of him. "I need to protect my investment."

Her dismay turned to revulsion. Did he mean her? What could he mean?

"I won't change my mind." A wave of tiredness came over her. She didn't want to have this argument, not now, not at this time of day. The thought of him being in Egypt was overwhelming and oppressive. "I know you care for me, Stephen, but I don't return your feelings. I won't marry you. Not now. Not ever."

Stephen's face darkened. He stalked toward her slowly, looming in front of her. "You will. I promise you." She backed away from him, feeling threatened, and her back hit against the bookcase with a soft thud. "You're mine. And you always will be."

Pinning her shoulders against the bookcase with a forearm across her clavicle, he grabbed her chin roughly in his fingertips. His mouth descended upon hers with a force that made her heart hammer into her chest. Paralyzing fear froze her. His lips moved against hers and she felt the clash of his teeth against her lips, his breath on her face.

His hands cupped her breasts, fondling her through the

fabric. His touch was enough to spur her into action. She reached for the closest book, fished it from the shelf with a shaking hand, then slammed the spine into the side of his head.

Stephen swore and sprang back. He touched the side of his head where she'd hit him, then inspected his fingers as though expecting to find blood. She wished she had hit him so hard. Hopefully she'd given him a good bruise, at least.

The book clattered to the floor as she ripped herself away from the bookcase, scrubbing her lips with her fingertips. "How dare you?" Her voice rippled with fury. The taste of his cigarettes remained on her lips, and she wanted nothing more than to go and bathe and rid herself of any trace of the repulsive kiss. "I'll—"

"You'll what?" Stephen's eyes narrowed. "Tell your father? Henry? And you don't think they'd only see your lewd behavior as more reason for you to marry me? Careful, dearest Ginny. If you admit too freely how I've spoiled you, you may not like the consequence. Everyone knows we've spent the summer together. And you've just told David Peterson you intend to marry me. You think anyone will believe you?"

Her lewd behavior? As though she'd invited it. Sickened, she swallowed back bile. "Get out," she gritted through clenched teeth.

Stephen glowered at her. "This isn't over."

He left and she sank onto the floor, struggling for breath, hands shaking.

His threats sliced into her skin and she relived the horrible kiss all over again.

She thought she'd disliked him before. Now, hatred ran through her veins.

CHAPTER TWELVE

*T*he door frame shook as the door opened and her father strode through into the breakfast room. Ginger set her teacup on the table slowly. She felt her face drain of color at the fury in her father's expression. All of it was directed at her. From her seat at the head of the table, Madeline tilted her head over her newspaper.

"What did you do?" Her father's face was red.

How had he learned of it so quickly? Both Madeline and Henry had promised not to tell her father before she had a chance to—and they were the only ones she'd told.

Had Stephen called her father to complain?

Henry stood from his place beside her. "Father—this isn't the time. It's been a hard morning for Ginny."

"Difficult because she made it so." Her father paced behind her chair. "You refused Stephen?"

"Yes." Ginger set her hands on the edge of the table in front of her. "I thought about it—as I promised I would—and decided I would rather die an old maid than marry Stephen." After his unwelcome kiss this morning, she no longer felt even the slightest guilt at refusing him.

A vein in her father's neck twitched. "And that's it then? That's all the answer he's to expect from you?"

Madeline folded her newspaper. "Really, Edmund, you're being too hard on the girl. She has a right to refuse offers she deems unsuitable."

"Frankly, this is none of your business," her father snapped.

Ginger cringed. She'd never seen her father be rude to her aunt like this, even if he didn't have the best opinion of her politics.

Madeline lifted her chin. "Odd that you should say that while standing in my house." She buttered a roll but kept her gaze leveled at her father.

"Don't test my patience, Madeline. I wouldn't be surprised in the slightest if you put these radical notions in Virginia's head. First, she declares her interest in becoming a nurse and now she rejects the best offer of marriage likely to ever come her way." Her father stopped his pacing and stood behind Ginger's chair. "You're making a mistake."

"The way I see it," Madeline said, rising from her seat, "it's you who's making the mistake, Edmund. You're alienating your daughter by insisting she marry your choice for her. But it's not your decision to make. And if you can't see how her desire to be a nurse isn't radically different from her lack of desire to marry Stephen Fisher, then you're a fool."

"Well, she'll never have my blessing for that ridiculous plan now." Her father stormed toward the door. "You hear me, Virginia? I will make sure no program will accept you. Now hurry and finish your breakfast—we have a train to catch. Thank you for your hospitality, Madeline. I'll take my leave of you now. No need to see us off. I've already told the servants to pack our things."

"My, what a temper," Madeline remarked, watching the

door her father had left through. "Nothing like a little morning indigestion."

"I'm sorry, aunt." Ginger closed her eyes, her head aching. The hours of sleep she'd lost in the morning already made thinking clearly difficult—not to mention the confrontation with Stephen. "He behaved like a beast."

"Do stay here for a few days, my dear. Some time in the city may do you some good. I'd hate to see you return on a train with Edmund when he's in such a foul mood. He might hem and haw all he'd like, but you're a grown woman. He can't really stop you from spending a few more days with your family."

Henry's mouth set to a line as he adjusted his collar. If he'd been angry with Ginger for telling Stephen no, he hadn't said so. That, at least, had been a relief. "I agree with Madeline. You should give Father some days to adjust to the news."

She didn't see why her father was taking it so hard. He liked Stephen but there were plenty of other rich young men out there. Still, Stephen had said something about going to Egypt to protect his investment. Was it possible there was something more with Stephen's business relationship than was evident?

As Henry sat once again, Ginger touched the crook of his arm. "And you? Does my decision upset you?"

Henry hesitated in his response, but the weary look in his face gave the impression of being far less impartial than he had suggested. "I support your decision. You have the right to choose whom you will marry. But it makes me worry you seem to think and act unilaterally, Ginny."

Madeline bristled in her seat. "It's not as though she's chosen to run off with a man far beneath her class, Harry. She's simply said 'no' to one offer."

Henry's lips tightened, wrinkling the skin around his

mouth. Then he said, "And an offer which might impact the woman I'm in love with."

Madeline rolled her eyes. "Oh, Harry, then do attach to someone else. Angelica is a flighty girl, without an ounce of brain in her blonde head. At least Charlotte Thompson had spirit and wit."

Ginger stiffened. Only Madeline would give voice to a sentiment they all shared. She held back a smile.

Henry didn't appear amused, though. A shadow crossed his face.

The subject would never cease to be a sore one with Henry, Ginger suspected. He winced, then put a hand over his vest as he stood. "That may be. But I care for Angelica. And I may be more prone to falling in love than my sister, but I also do everything with a great deal of consideration as to how it will affect her—and the rest of my family."

Henry left the two women with a slight bow. A lump rose in the back of Ginger's throat, a dark feeling of gloom enclosing her heart. "I've disappointed him."

Madeline leaned forward in her seat and reached for Ginger's hand. "You are not a disappointment. We're women. Our situation is not as easy as men like to pretend it is—particularly when it's such a struggle to do anything without their permission. I may not understand your choice, my dear, but this is your decision. Your father and brother's opinions are irrelevant."

"To be honest, it's more difficult to disappoint Henry than Papa. Henry at least has tried to be impartial, even though I know he isn't. My father has ignored the many times I've told him I'm uncomfortable with Stephen's particular brand of love." Ginger sighed, not feeling any appetite for the breakfast set before her. She was tempted to tell Madeline of Stephen's earlier assault but fear tightened around her chest. "Is it really all right if I stay with you for some days?"

Madeline nodded. "I just wish Meg was here to keep you company. I'm afraid I'm not nearly as exciting as she is. But perhaps Gran and I can come up with some interesting ways of keeping your mind from the heaviness of your heart."

It would also give her the opportunity to visit Charlie Martin. Perhaps even spend some time with James Clark. That alone made her spirits feel lighter. She smiled. "Thank you, aunt. Though after breakfast I need to find Henry and smooth things over with him before he goes to Somerset. And do try not to mention Charlotte to him. Any talk of her still seems to set his teeth on edge."

Madeline put her forefinger and thumb to her lips and twisted them as though she was turning a key in a lock. "Mum's the word. I shan't mention her again. Now," Madeline held up her copy of the *Daily Sketch* "have you heard of this marvelous dog that has been carrying coded messages in Belgium? The things they think of! They've apparently trained the creature to act as a carrier pigeon."

"And the Germans haven't just shot the poor thing?" Ginger leaned toward the newspaper to look at the image of the dog. "It seems a rather precarious thing to put his image in the papers."

"Well, they can't start killing every dog they see."

As they turned toward other topics, Ginger felt herself relax. She was glad the confrontation with Stephen had taken place here at her aunt's house, rather than at Penmore. Even though her mother was similar to her sister, her mother was more likely to take her father's side.

And without Stephen's proposal, her future felt clearer. She would go to Egypt with her family, which she wanted to do, anyway. She longed to explore all the antiquities which had fascinated her so much as a girl, and work on her Arabic, too.

If only Stephen wasn't promising to haunt her there, as well.

Ginger remembered Stephen's hands on her breasts and gave a sudden jolt. Shuddering, she clenched her teeth, feeling the taint of his touch again. She had to find a way to be rid of him. Would Henry help her?

When she'd finished breakfast, Ginger went in search of her brother. She found him upstairs, dressing for the journey home. Henry excused the valet and Ginger came in and sat on the bed.

Henry surveyed his appearance in the mirror and adjusted his cufflinks. "What is it?"

Ginger leaned against the stiff wooden post on the four-poster bed. "I don't want you to leave for Penmore with any tension between us. You've risked life and limb for me the past few days, and I'm not trying to be ungrateful."

"I know." Henry ran his hands over the front of his vest. "I expect I'll be exchanging this for my uniform in the coming days. But don't exaggerate the danger. While I took risks, they were quite by accident."

"You're braver than you let on." Ginger set her hands on either side of her on the bed and leaned back. "Did Stephen give you the details of John Martin's naturalization after he left me?"

Henry shook his head. "No...though I can't say I want to ask him about it now. He left before I spoke with him again. And if he took the news as badly as you say, I don't want him to feel I've abused our friendship."

"I'm not sure I can avoid it." She scrunched her face with guilt. "He accused me of that. And I asked him about the details as best I could before he left—though I think he wanted to strike me for it. He says David Peterson has set up the naturalization for five days from now. But you must get some paperwork to get him out of prison first."

Henry sighed. "I'll give it a couple of days and then ring Stephen to get the details sorted. If you don't mind. Much as it may have been foolish of me, I really do care for Angelica. I don't want to do anything more to threaten my standing with her right now."

She stared at him, her mouth feeling dry. If she told him about the way Stephen had assaulted her, it might mean yet another threat to his relationship with Angelica. If Henry confronted Stephen, what would it mean for Henry's hopes with the girl?

How many times in the last few days had she told her family that Henry's relationship with Angelica was more of a solution to the security of Penmore than her engagement with Stephen?

She couldn't rely on Henry to help her with this.

Not without doing more damage.

She gritted her teeth, blinking back the sheen of tears threatening her. No wonder Stephen had felt so free to do whatever he wanted to her.

But she had to do *something* to put a wedge between her and Stephen. Just not with Henry's help.

Her voice felt scratchy as she finally answered Henry. "I don't mind if you take some time before talking to Stephen about John Martin. Just don't forget about it." She stood, her arms swinging as she sauntered over to him and planted a kiss on his cheek. "Thank you for being such a good big brother."

"Hmmm, I try. Though you wouldn't let me forget the Martins even if I could." Henry chuckled and then ruffled her hair, just slightly, as he used to do when she was a girl.

She jerked backward with a tight smile, trying to pretend nothing was amiss. "Don't make more work for poor Violet. I'm already going to have to send her to unpack my things again."

His eyes gleamed and then he quirked an eyebrow. "Yes, poor Violet. We should give any maid that has to deal with you and Lucy a raise."

Ginger shrugged. "I can agree with the part about Lucy." She clasped his hand. "I'm glad we can be friends again before you leave. Can you try to fix things with father for me? Convince him that joining the nurses will be a good thing?"

"I can't say Madeline has done you any favors with the matter. Just be careful, Ginny. I don't see this situation with father getting better if you continue to press the issue. Can you let this idea go? You've done quite a lot of crusading the last few days. You may have to sacrifice some things you want."

Henry's lack of support stung, but didn't surprise her. She swallowed, hard and gave him a stiff nod. If he only knew she'd just sacrificed her own dignity and pride for his sake.

As she left him, she pressed a hand over her heart, taking a slow, shallow breath. She'd gone to Henry, hoping to find the security and comfort she'd always expected from him. Now she felt more alone than ever.

CHAPTER THIRTEEN

"There's a telephone call for you, Lady Virginia," Giles announced from the doorway to the sitting room.

Ginger looked up from the settee, where she and Gran had been in the middle of a card game. After her father and Henry had left for the train station an hour earlier, Madeline had called Gran over for a visit.

A telephone call at Penmore was a rare enough event. Who would call her here at her aunt's? Ginger frowned and set her hand down, the cards silkily shuffling into a pile. "Who is it?"

"A Mr. David Peterson, my lady. He asked for your brother first, but since I informed him he was no longer here, he asked for you instead." Giles held the door for her.

David Peterson? Even though he'd helped her, Ginger felt a chill go up her spine at his name. He was Stephen's friend. Maybe Stephen had told him of her refusal. He could be angry Ginger had tricked him. She excused herself from her grandmother and went into the foyer, where the telephone stood on the console table.

She took the earpiece and then leaned into the heavy mouthpiece. "This is Virginia Whitman."

"Lady Virginia. David Peterson." The voice on the line crackled with static, sounding as though it came from a tin box. "Where on earth is John Martin? If he doesn't arrive in the next hour, I'm afraid the opportunity will completely pass us over."

"John Martin?" Ginger went rigid with shock. But Stephen had said...

She remembered the distant look in his eyes when she'd asked.

He'd given her the wrong date.

"I'm so sorry, Mr. Peterson. My brother left an hour ago —where is it he's supposed to be getting John Martin from? Perhaps I can meet him there and see if there's been a hiccup." She motioned to Giles to get her paper and a pen, which he supplied immediately.

David rattled off an address. "But it's not likely it'll do you any good to go there. Stephen delivered the paperwork to Henry himself. Without it, he won't be able to get out of the internment camp."

She didn't believe for one second Stephen had given Henry the paperwork. Henry would have said something.

Ginger stared at the address. It was in the city. "John is here in London?"

David's voice crackled. "Yes, it's a former factory of some sort. It's being used for the interned. But he must be here within the hour."

Was it possible she could get him from the internment center herself? Even without the paperwork?

"Could you stall for any longer, Mr. Peterson? I hate to ask—"

He released a guttural sigh. "Perhaps by a few minutes, but it isn't likely. I'll do my utmost."

Ginger hung up the receiver and stared at the address she'd scrawled. The paper shook in her hands, a mixture of fury and fear running through her.

Of all the cold-hearted, horrible things for Stephen to do. He'd done it on purpose. Maybe revenge—or to teach her how much she "needed" him.

She rushed back to the sitting room in a daze.

Gran and Madeline stared at her expectantly, and then Gran tilted her head, clearly reading her distress. "Something tells me David Peterson was not the bearer of good news."

"No, he's—" Ginger rubbed her temple, a dull, brutal pain pulsing through the top of her head. A sudden headache. Or she just hadn't noticed it before. She slackened her jaw, sure she'd been clenching it, and met her grandmother's eyes. "He's just informed me Stephen gave me the wrong date for John Martin's naturalization. Henry was supposed to have him at Mr. Peterson's office right now."

Madeline and Gran exchanged a look. "And what does that mean?" Madeline asked, arching a brow.

"It means—" Ginger released a deep breath "—it means Stephen lied to me when I asked him about the details. I'd say it was a cruel joke, but he'll probably claim to have been so broken-hearted by my refusal he simply mixed up the date. And if John Martin isn't at the Home Secretary's office within the hour, the opportunity will be gone."

"But why?" Gran leaned forward. "Surely if they'll naturalize him today, they can naturalize him some other day."

Would they though? David Peterson had been quite firm about the deadline.

"Stephen arranged the whole matter—by using some of his father's connections. I'm certain those connections won't be at my disposal now. And even if they were, who's to say Stephen won't undo the arrangement to get his revenge with me? Mr. Peterson probably hasn't heard I've refused Stephen yet—but he himself was doing me the favor under the impression he was doing a favor for Stephen's fiancée." Ginger crumpled the address into her fist, her hand shaking.

She paced, agitated and furious. "I must get John Marin out of the internment center myself. That's all there is to it." She whirled in a circle, then stormed from the room, heading for the stairwell.

A rush of footsteps sounded behind her. "What are you going to do?" Madeline asked.

Gran and Madeline had followed and were mere steps away. Their concern was evident—and something more . . . *Are they willing to help?*

Ginger started up the stairs. "I don't know. I'll think of something along the way."

Gran's voice grew louder. "I always say, if you can't win fairly...cheat." Ginger stopped and looked back. Gran gave her a stern look.

Ginger unwrinkled the paper. John Martin wasn't terribly far. She'd need a car—and a reason to get him out of the internment camp. But she doubted she could simply go to the camp and demand they release him.

He needed a reason to leave.

She stomped her foot. "This is why I need to learn to do something useful with my life. Everyone can guffaw all they want about my wish to be a nurse, but when situations like this arrive, it would be nice to be capable of more than nothing." She stopped short, her chin jerking upright.

"Ah, look, Mama, it seems our darling Ginger has had an idea." Madeline's green gaze gleamed.

"She has." Gran marched closer. "Out with it."

"Do you think—" Ginger came back down the stairs toward them. "Would they allow John Martin out of the internment center for a medical reason? If a doctor, for example, were to say he was transferring him for treatment to the hospital?"

"They might." Madeline looked skeptical. "But we'd need a doctor."

Ginger smiled. "I might know one willing to help."

* * *

GINGER BOUNCED HER KNEE NERVOUSLY, her heart jittery as the car drew closer to St. Thomas' Hospital. She wished for a pocket watch. Anything to let her know how much time she had left. On her lap, she held the uniforms the matron of nurses had lent her. She'd grabbed them before she left, thinking if she needed an excuse to speak to James, returning the uniforms might be a good one.

Gran put her hand on Ginger's knee. She and Madeline had insisted on coming with her—though Ginger wasn't certain if it was a good thing or not. Gran could slow her. Giving her a sardonic smile, Gran said, "Really, Ginger. You're not jumping rope, there's no need to bounce."

"I'm sorry, Gran, I'm nervous." Ginger sucked in a slow, calming breath, her chest tight. "What if James doesn't agree to it? I'm probably asking him to do something illegal."

"You said he's a Liberal. They're always more than happy to disregard propriety." Gran shrugged and patted the silver curls of her head exposed below her hat.

Madeline laughed. "Oh, Mama—don't let Hugh hear you say it. He voted with the Liberals recently."

"Yes." Gran made a face of distaste. "But Hugh isn't here. The only way he'll hear it is if you're foolish enough to tell him."

The car stopped in front of the hospital. Ginger scrambled from her seat before the chauffer climbed out. "Stay here," she told her aunt and grandmother. "It'll be faster if I go alone."

She bundled the uniforms under her arm and hurried into the entrance. Somehow within a few days of visiting the hospital, she'd learned the route well. She was usually terrible with directions.

Racing up the staircase to the floor where James' office was, she prayed he'd be there.

She reached his office, her heart pounding through her blouse. She knocked, trying to catch her breath.

He didn't answer.

She tried the knob, but the door appeared to be locked.

Her heart falling, Ginger turned. Where could he be?

Footsteps approached and Ginger grew hopeful. But as the sound drew closer, an orderly rounded the corner, not James.

"Excuse me," Ginger called out to him. "Would you know where Dr. Clark is?"

"He's in surgery, miss." The orderly gave her a polite nod. "Don't expect he'll be out soon, but you can wait for him on that bench if you'd like."

Disappointment crushed her core.

Without James' help, she had no backup plan. She couldn't very well pretend to be a doctor credibly, even if there were women doctors in London.

...but she could pretend to be a nurse.

She stared at the uniforms in her hands.

Would she be believable? Maybe. But her chances were better still if she had sister nurses with her.

* * *

CLIMBING BACK into Madeline's car, Ginger handed the uniforms to her aunt before settling into her seat. She'd

changed into the one walking-about uniform the matron had
lent her—a uniform meant for use on the nurses' days off. As
it was more fitted than the others, changing in the hospital
had seemed like the best option.

"What on earth?" Madeline stared at the outfit Ginger
wore. She rifled through the stack of uniforms Ginger had
given her. "What's all this?"

"QA uniforms. I have a new plan. Dr. Clark is in surgery.
Since you came with me, you're going to help me. Get
dressed." Ginger pulled the stack from Madeline's lap and
sorted the uniforms, handing them one each. "They're large
enough that you can pull them over your dresses, however
uncomfortable it may be. They're ward dresses and aprons.
I'm not certain how to fix the veil, but I'm sure between the
three of us we can make sense of it. I have one for myself
here."

Gran stared at her as though she had gone mad. "You're
expecting me to don one of those—sacks? While riding in the
backseat of this motorcar?"

"Precisely." Ginger grinned, stretching the veil out in
front of her. *How is this thing supposed to go?* "I'm not sure if I
can convince them of anything on my own. But who would
question three noble nurses of the Queen Alexandra's? Especially when one is as mature and wise as you, Gran." Her
grandmother's eyes narrowed. "Where's your sense of adventure? A man's life is on the line."

"Exaggeration won't help you, dearest. Don't think I
haven't noticed you called me old. I'm not a relic." Her grandmother had been a young mother and proud that she wasn't
as old as some of the other women in her circles. Gran held
up the ward dress as though it was an infant's dirty nappy.
"Did you steal these?"

"Borrowed would be a better term for it." At Gran's
uplifted brow, Ginger said, "The QA matron allowed me to

borrow them, in fact, to see about having some tailored. Normally they wouldn't do it before an applicant was accepted, but Dr. Clark had a hand in persuading her."

"I think it's quite resourceful." Madeline gave a chuckle. She tapped on the window for the chauffer to pull forward, back onto the road.

Madeline pulled the ward dress over her blouse. It was a rather shapeless greyish blue sack. As she buttoned it, Ginger noticed her watching her grandmother. Would they be able to convince her?

Gran glowered as Madeline pulled on the apron. "You look ridiculous."

"Oh, pretend you're an actress, Mama. Here, I'll help you." Madeline scooted across her seat toward her.

Gran held up her hands. "No, thank you. I'm quite capable of pulling a potato sack over my head." She removed her hat. "I suppose I'm to rid myself of all my jewelry, as well?"

"If we're to be believable." Despite the humor of the situation, Ginger's nervous feeling grew more intense as they drew closer to the area of town where the Martins were being interned.

By the time they arrived, the three women had transformed themselves into nurses, as best they could. Ginger's laugh was a temporary relief to the growing tension in her chest. "Thank you for this. I'll never forget it."

"Oh, believe me—I won't let you." Gran harrumphed as the chauffer pulled up in front of the factory. "Perhaps the only reason I'm doing this, you should know, is because I'm proud you had the spine to stand up to your father over that awful Stephen Fisher. But no one is ever to know of this, understood?"

Several military and police officials milled outside the building and Ginger tried to settle her trembling hands.

What if they were caught? Her mother might not ever forgive her if Ginger was to blame for her grandmother and aunt being thrown in jail.

They stepped onto the pavement. Their shoes weren't right for the outfits. But little could be done about it and Ginger prayed no one would notice. Despite the urge to laugh at their appearance, as a police officer walked by them and frowned, she quickly sobered.

"Buck up," Madeline whispered in her ear. "It's time to prove you're willing to take those risks you claim you are."

"I am," Ginger whispered back. "I worry about what happens to you and Gran if we're found out."

"We wouldn't be dressed like this if we minded," Gran remarked dryly. "Besides which. I rather like to think you got this penchant for trouble from me. It skipped Elizabeth entirely. I'm glad to see it alive and strong. Never forget. You're a Scot on this side of the family. We Scots do as we please."

Ginger held back a laugh.

Taking charge, Ginger made her way down the pavement to what appeared to be the front entrance. By the time they reached it, she was drenched in sweat from the summer heat. Madeline and Gran were in a similar state, a sheen on their foreheads. Silver hairs stuck to Gran's forehead. Wearing two outfits must be intolerable.

A military officer stood at the entrance. "Yes, Sisters?"

"We're here for a medical transport," Ginger said, her voice sounding much more solid than she felt. In addition to the heat, her knees felt weak. She'd never done anything like this before.

He frowned and checked his clipboard. "I don't have a record of a medical transport."

Ginger hesitated and Gran stepped forward. "Young man. We have been sent from St. Thomas' Hospital to collect a patient who is desperately in need of quarantine. Immediately. His entire family has typhus. Now, are you going to be the one who allows the disease to spread among the inmates and officers because someone didn't give you the proper paperwork?"

Ginger held back an astonished look. Gran wasn't the type to allow herself to be pushed to the side, but her authoritative tone had been more convincing than Ginger would have imagined.

The officer reddened and shifted, as though feeling threatened by the idea of getting typhus himself. He scanned their faces. "I-I...let me see who I can talk to about this. What's the prisoner's name?"

"John Martin," Ginger said quickly. "This was supposed to have been arranged this morning, sir."

The officer nodded. "One moment, please."

As he slipped inside, Ginger gave her grandmother a side-long glance. "What on earth? How did you come up with all that?"

"Years of filling my brain with mysteries, I suppose." A smile twitched at her grandmother's lips.

"And Hugh said you'd gain nothing from novel reading," Madeline muttered with lifted brows.

The reverberating engines of motorcars and clopping of horse carriages on the street were a distant din. Escape seemed so far. No turning back now.

A familiar car pulled up beside the curb and Stephen stepped from it.

Turning away from him, Ginger felt her heartbeat pulse in her throat. "What in God's name is he doing here?" She set a hand on Madeline's to steady herself. He would recognize her in an instant.

"What is it?" Madeline looked over her shoulder. "Oh—" She nudged her mother. "Don't look now, Mama. We're about to get caught."

Gran glanced back and then gave them both a smug smile. "Don't look at him. He isn't likely to give us a moment's attention if we're not looking at him. He can't possibly recognize us from behind."

As Stephen drew closer, the officer came out the door again. "This way, please. You'll need to identify the patient. We have more than one man with that name here." He glanced past them at Stephen, who stopped behind them. "You'll have to wait a few minutes, sir. What're you here for?"

"I'm here to see the head of command. On a very urgent matter," Stephen said. Gran was right. He barely paid attention to them.

"As soon as I'm done helping these sisters." The officer held the door for them.

Ginger passed through, her gait feeling stiff and artificial. *Just remain calm.* She felt faint and breathed shallowly, gripping Madeline's arm.

Why was Stephen here? To reverse the paperwork he'd obtained for John Martin?

She wouldn't put it past him.

The air inside was degrees cooler but nothing helped the insufferable feeling of choking. They followed the officer to what appeared to be some sort of holding room. Another officer sat at a desk, drinking tea as he wrote in a ledger. As they arrived, a back door in the room opened and John came through, accompanied by an escort. Two other interned men filed in behind him.

"That's him. That's the patient." Ginger moved toward John. She pointed to him. The officer gave him a wary look.

John appeared dumbfounded but from the way he drew in his eyebrows, he recognized her.

Ginger met his gaze, giving him a pleading look. *Please*

don't give us away. Her voice felt hoarse as she spoke, "This is the man who needs to be in quarantine."

John blanched. "Quarantine?"

"Your family has come down with typhus. We have medical transport for you. We need to leave immediately," Madeline said in a stern tone.

Gran gave a grave nod.

John shifted nervously. "Typhus? Well what about—"

His father? Of course, that would be the worry. Ginger cut him off. "Please, Mr. Martin. Don't give us any trouble. This whole internment center is at risk if you don't cooperate and come along. You wouldn't want to put everyone in danger, would you?" She had to hope the officers didn't know the internees well enough to know John also had a father here.

John's face was somber. The officer at the desk shifted in his seat, holding his mug back as though the disease could be transmitted through it. "Is my family all right?" John asked.

"We're taking care of them." Hopefully that would be enough for him to understand she was trying to help him. Ginger took a deep breath, wanting more than anything to tell John the truth. She wished she could see Mr. Martin. Promise she would keep fighting for him. Give him a chance to say goodbye to his son. She hoped John would forgive her for not letting her have a chance to say goodbye.

Gran and Madeline were at her side. "Quickly now," Madeline said and held her arm out for John to take. The officer at the desk wore a bewildered but resigned expression. "We'll return him when he's well. Thank you, officer."

They hurried out the door to the holding room, the front guard still escorting them. Before it shut, Ginger gave one last glance back.

She wanted more than anything to help Mr. Martin, too.

Henry's voice rang in her head. *Friedrich is beyond our help. You must accept that.*

She didn't want to accept it.

Drawing closer to the front guard's station, Ginger saw Stephen through a window. He still waited outside, a scowl on his face. Going out this way would mean he'd see her for sure.

"Not this way." Ginger spun toward the guard. "We don't want to put any member of the public at risk by getting too close. Is there a back entrance?"

The guard took several steps away, rubbing his hands on his jacket uneasily. He nodded. "But isn't it better to just get him outside?"

"Could you, perhaps, escort that man in the front elsewhere? It would be for the best," Madeline said. "Then we can go through once you're both safely out of the way."

The guard gave a brisk nod, clearly relieved to be away from the diseased patient. He hurried out. Moments later, he and Stephen started off in another direction.

Ginger held her breath as they went outside. The closer they drew to the car, the more her heart pounded.

Madeline's chauffer said nothing as he opened the door to the motorcar for them. But a smile glimmered in his eyes.

As the door shut behind them, Ginger gripped the sides of her seat, her palms sweating.

Somehow, they'd done it.

CHAPTER FOURTEEN

Standing in the back of the hospital ward at St. Thomas', Ginger watched as John sat beside Charlie. Her joy felt incomplete. But at least John would be free. And as a British subject, it meant help for Mrs. Martin and her children. He would stay in London and help with his brother's recovery. Her aunt had promised to help with Charlie's care and to find John lodging and food.

Until the British Army called him away to the service he'd promised himself to.

A small part of her wondered if he wouldn't have been safer staying in internment.

James approached her and crossed his arms as he stood at her side, watching John. "And how is it you accomplished this?"

She gave him a slight smile. "I broke the rules." At his curious look, she added, "I may have gone to the internment center and told them his family had typhus and he needed to be quarantined. By the by, you wouldn't be willing to discreetly return some nursing uniforms for me? I may have used them."

James' mouth opened in shock. "You didn't."

"It wasn't just me. My aunt and grandmother helped. In fact, Gran came up with the typhus claim. She was brilliant."

His incredulousness seemed to deepen, his eyes wide. "Now I know where you get your spirit from."

Ginger laughed, covering her face as embarrassment crept in around her chest. "I don't know that I'll ever forget it."

"Then they support you joining the nursing service?"

"Not entirely." Ginger tilted her head and indicated they should leave the ward. "John's naturalization was at stake. We had to get him to the Home Office but had a limited window to do it and lacked the proper paperwork." She didn't want to tell him about Stephen, or how she'd come to him for help.

James stopped walking and shook his head, admiration shining in his eyes. "You truly are an incredible woman, Ginger."

"Thank you." She laughed. "You flatter me. I'm much more selfish than you give me credit for."

"Well, I don't see that at all. I see a kind, brave woman who would do her country proud as a nurse." He cleared his throat. "And, I might add, that any man would be proud to have as his fiancée."

A fiancée?

She really hadn't been paying attention to James, had she?

He'd helped her, introduced her to his mother. Inspired her to consider new opportunities.

What if this was the type of man she'd been looking for? She didn't care for him the way she thought she might—but romance could blossom. After all, she didn't really know what love was. Her father had pointed that out to her more than once.

Ginger met his earnest expression and a thrill of excitement rose in her. Gran's words echoed in her mind:

If you can't win fairly...cheat.

Her father had said he wanted her engagement settled before she entered the nursing training program. But he hadn't said to whom.

EPILOGUE

*P*enmore loomed in front of Ginger as the car made its way up the drive. Beside her, Violet beamed. "Aren't you glad to be home, my lady?"

The knot of tension in Ginger's chest tightened. She'd timed the trip home precisely, after spending a week at Madeline's. The announcement would be in the newspaper this morning. Her father may have already seen it.

Sneaking John Martin out of an internment center seemed easy compared to this. Not to mention that she wouldn't have her aunt or grandmother at her side.

"Delighted." Ginger even managed a taut smile.

God, help me.

The car stopped in a cloud of dust. She released a restrained breath.

Her mother and Mr. Pierce met her outside. Her mother's hands were clasped in front of her, her expression placid.

But one look was enough for Ginger to be certain.

She knew.

Ginger stepped out onto the gravel and hurried toward

her mother. "Good morning, Mama." She took her mother's
proffered hands and kissed her cheek, lightly.

Her mother pulled back and her mouth twisted. "I can't
say it's been a very good morning for me, Ginger."

Ginger grimaced, her gaze flicking toward the window of
her father's study. "Is he very angry?"

Sighing, her mother's arms drooped by her sides. "I don't
know that 'angry' is the right word for it. He wants to see
you. Straight away."

"Are you coming with me?" Ginger asked her mother as
Violet disappeared into the house with her bag. Ginger
wished she could go with the maid. She didn't really know
where Violet was headed—she'd never paid attention. But
the gates of hell seemed preferable right now to facing the
wrath of her father.

Her mother shook her head. "He wants to speak to you
alone. He's in his study." She rubbed her temple, as though
she was fighting a headache. "I know you didn't want to
marry Stephen, but this? You don't know this man. And
we've never even met the fellow. I thought you wanted
love."

Ginger swallowed the lump in her throat. "Father left me
no other option. I wouldn't normally have rushed into an
arrangement like this, but I want to be a nurse for the war,
Mama, and Father—"

"Yes, your father told me all about it." The gravel
crunched under her mother's shoes as she shifted her weight.
"I understand why you've done this, but Ginger, you've been
gently bred. What you'll see in this war will stay with you
forever." Biting her lip, her mother added, "Do yourself the
favor of convincing your father this man is everything you've
been claiming you want. I've done what I could to help. The
rest is up to you."

The darkness beyond the front door seemed cold,

uninviting. A week of carefully cultivating a plan hadn't been enough.

A lifetime wouldn't be enough. She'd always be frightened, always feel she wouldn't get it right.

The walk to her father's study felt interminable. Though she couldn't see them, she was certain she felt the eyes of the household on her. James had wanted to come with her. He'd been worried that making the announcement without asking her father for her hand would be too bold a step.

She couldn't explain to him his proposal wouldn't be welcome no matter how properly he offered it. This was the easier way.

Opening the door to the study, she found her father at his desk. He didn't move as she approached and stopped beside him. A map of Egypt was laid out on the desktop. His hands were on either side of the map, his head bent in concentration.

"Getting ready for the trip?" Ginger finally said. His refusal to look at her didn't bode well.

He nodded and drummed his fingers on the desk. "Did you hear?"

"Hear what?" she asked, feeling more off-balance than before.

"Friedrich Martin was repatriated. Sent to Germany two days ago." His fingers cracked as he clenched and unclenched a fist. "I thought you'd be interested to find out."

Her heart fell. *No...* She'd been worried. Especially after she'd seen Stephen at the internment center. *That bastard.* She was sure he'd been behind it. Thank goodness she'd been able to save John from a similar fate. At least she hadn't completely failed.

"Did—how is Mrs. Martin?" she managed. A sick feeling clenched in her gut.

"As one might expect. But she's grateful you helped her

son. Both of them. Calls you her guardian angel." Her father still hadn't met her gaze.

"It must have been Stephen." Ginger folded her hands in front of her. "I saw him at the detention center after I finally turned him down. I'm certain he had a hand in having Mr. Martin repatriated with speed." She lifted her chin. "And what's more—Stephen attempted to take liberties with me. You ought to know what sort of man he is, in case you still believe he's worthy of me."

"Liberties?" Her father gave her a sharp look, one that burned her to her core.

"Yes, well, I fought him off." This wasn't the sort of conversation she would ever feel comfortable having with her father.

"Then you'd be wise not to speak of it to anyone." His eyes were hard and flat.

So much for protecting me.

Her father's reaction oddly didn't disappoint her with the acute pain she felt she ought to have expected. How long had she spent telling him that Stephen wasn't right for her? Too long. And he'd insisted all the same. Whatever was blinding her father in this way was something she couldn't change. He'd thrown his lot in with Stephen, perhaps for Henry's sake.

And his son and heir was ultimately less expendable that his troublesome daughter.

Her heart panged with the thought.

Her father folded the map over, revealing the open newspaper underneath it. Her engagement announcement was on display below it. "Care to explain this?"

Had he led with the terrible news about Mr. Martin to unnerve her?

Her mouth was dry. "You met him in London—the doctor who cared for—"

"Yes, I know who the fellow is. That's not the point."

"I love him." Not the whole truth, but she didn't dare say any differently to her father. The thought of James made her happy. That was enough. It might not be the passionate excitement she'd once believed possible, but who knew if that even existed. "We're compatible. He's a good man, from a fine family. His parents are delighted."

"He should have come to me." Her father stood straighter. "This...running around, behind my back—"

"There was nothing inappropriate in this, Father. And you can find no flaw with the man. He may not have Stephen Fisher's wealth, but he'll be a fine husband. And he's willing to wait until after the war to be wed."

"After the war?" The surprise in her father's face was evident.

She counted her heartbeat by the soft ticking of the grandfather clock in the study. "Yes. I'm going to join the Queen Alexandra's. You said I had to be engaged and I am. I spoke to the matron and she's agreed to send me to Egypt for my post after my training. In fact, James is going to request the RAMC send him there, as well."

"The Queen Alexandra's..." Her father's anger burned in his eyes. He pointed toward her. "You're young and naïve. You know nothing of war. Nothing of how inhumane men can be toward one another. You think the situation with the Martins was a travesty? You'll see soon enough. You'll even learn to hate in a way you never thought possible."

His shoulders sank as he squared off with her, his mouth set to a line.

At last, he gave a curt nod. "You've made a worthy adversary, Virginia. Beaten your father at his game, as it were."

"It's not about that—"

His laugh was sardonic. "Isn't it though?" He folded the

newspaper and thrust it in her hands. "Have your doctor. And your nursing. But don't think I'll ever trust you again."

Then he walked out the door, leaving her alone in his study.

Ginger braced herself against his desk, her emotions jumbled.

He'd said yes.

Yes.

Tears welled in her eyes and she covered her mouth, a choked, joyful laugh caught in her throat.

He would let her be a nurse. And she and James would be married.

The map on the desk promised something else...

Egypt awaited.

She sank back into her father's chair, where she'd crawled as a girl to take shelter among the books and the sturdy scent of her home. The old leather was soft and worn and she ran her fingertips along the cracks in the grain.

...don't think I'll ever trust you again...

Nothing would ever be the same.

AUTHOR'S NOTE

First, let's talk about the thing that I fibbed to you about: Kitchener's face on a poster. The truth is that famous design didn't appear until September of 1914, but my editors and I decided it would be a shame not to include it, so there it is. Since this is a work of fiction, I occasionally take liberty with some facts and that's one of them. *Mea culpa.*

As for the other historical events depicted in this novel, they were sadly, altogether too true. The Aliens Restriction Act was passed the day after Britain declared war on Germany. To be fair, this type of law wasn't exclusive to Britain and not the first law of its kind to be passed. Even in our present day, there continues to be a backlash against ethnic groups of the opposing side and their innocent civilian populations during war.

That's why I focused on and chose to highlight its effects on helpless women and families caught in the crossfire, particularly like the fictional Mrs. Martin. Their sad tales included permanent separations from their spouses and fathers, some of whom were repatriated to Germany and never heard from again.

The early 20th century saw the backlash of the nationalist movements that had started in the late 19th century. The exuberance at the declaration of war is also documented and true. At the time, the citizen nationals saw the war as an opportunity for their country to shine. Of course, no one quite knew what they were in for.

The effect of this nationalistic fervor continued to affect both policy and diplomacy as the war went on, which provides the backdrop of the Windswept WWI Saga. As the adventure moves to Egypt and Middle East, this sense of nationalism took a particularly vicious turn in imperialistic folly which shaped the modern world and created some of the most controversial political decisions in history. I hope you'll join Ginger in her adventures in the deserts of Egypt and Arabia, where she'll face grueling adversity and be swept away in an epic romance.

Thanks for reading!

NOW AVAILABLE

WINDSWEPT
Book 1
The Windswept WWI Saga

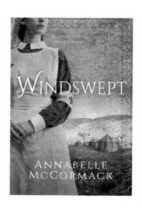

1917. When British nurse Ginger Whitman finds a wounded enemy soldier hiding in her hospital camp in Palestine, she knows she should turn him in. But he's desperate and dying —and he claims he's a spy with a message about a critical plot against British forces.

Then the arrival of mysterious intelligence officer Major Noah Benson offers a chance of help. But Noah is as charming as he is dangerous and Ginger's heart is at risk. With a deadly enemy hunting her, Ginger is caught in a crossfire of secrets and lies. Trusting the wrong person could do more than cost her life: it could change the course of the war.

Windswept is the first novel in the Windswept WWI Saga. A story of spies, family drama, romance, and epic adventure, it is set in the British Middle Eastern front of the First World War. **This novel contains violence and romantic, steamy moments.**

Purchase Windswept and continue Ginger Whitman's story today!

Read on for a look into the first chapter of *Windswept*.

FIRST CHAPTER OF WINDSWEPT

MAY 1917

DEIR EL BELAH, PALESTINE

*W*eary of death, Ginger Whitman couldn't seem to drag herself away from it.

The dim light of dawn shrouded the path winding down the side of the craggy hill. Her boots slid on sand and rock as she loosened the clasp of her short red uniform cape, wiping the sweat on her neck. The stench of decay curdled in her throat.

A half-dozen soldiers worked. Their shovels scraped into sand with a thumping cadence. Each toss of earth devoured the broken bodies in the pits beside them. Some nurses called her foolish for coming here every morning. But who else would come to pay respects? She couldn't recognize the dead faces from her vantage point, but their voices haunted her dreams. Lives cut short by the unending, brutal tide of war.

The chaplain stood nearby, praying. She bowed her head. So many lives she couldn't help save. The bodies of Ottoman

Turks fallen on the British line received a similar hasty burial nearby. In death, the heaps of bodies were indistinguishable, save for the remnants of uniforms. Death made equals of cowards and heroes, friend or foe. As the war had progressed, the British government enacted sober policies for burying enemy dead. The government had more hope their enemies would return the favor than she did.

She lifted her hand to her nose, the rotten scent stoking her ire. Her father predicted when she'd joined that she'd learn to hate. He'd called her naïve, claimed when the pleasantries of polite society vanished, she would understand the safety she'd abandoned. He hadn't been entirely wrong—but what he labeled as safety had been innocence cloaked in the privilege of her family's wealth and status. Three years of lost innocence tormented her soul like a festering wound.

She muttered a prayer for the Turkish soldiers too.

As she kept watch, the grey hills transformed to vibrant yellows and baked white stone, dotted with verdant brush. The hillsides lush with vegetation, adjacent to the sea, draped Palestine with unexpected beauty. The now-impenetrable town of Gaza, where the Ottoman Turks held their ground through two costly battles, loomed in the distance. The British advance had stalled. The longer they stayed, Ginger detected an increasing sense of hopelessness in the men she treated.

A sharp sting pricked her forearm. She crushed the mosquito feasting there. She scratched the red welt—one of many. With May's heat growing stronger by the day, pests swarmed in hordes. If her mother knew the state of her skin, she'd faint.

Days before Ginger's debut into society, a blemish had erupted on her chin. Her mother had directed servants to comb the whole of Somerset for a poultice to make it disappear. The days when those things seemed important were laughable now. The world had turned upside down and, along with it, her carefully groomed role. Her mother's letters still brimmed with ideas for Ginger's planned wedding after the war. The thought of a wedding felt like a tether to another life.

Distant gunfire crackled across the ridges of the sand dunes. The troops entrenched a few miles away were starting early. Or some unfortunate soul had risked a cigarette and found a sniper's quick response. She hoped she was wrong. Quiet resumed, and she checked her wristwatch. Dread crept up her esophagus. She'd rather stay around the burial pits than return today.

She climbed the steep hill and stopped to regain her breath, tucking strands of her flame-red hair behind her ears and under her cap. She looked out over the tranquility of the rippling Mediterranean, then turned. Tens of thousands of horses, mules, and camels rested on the plain alongside men waiting for the chance to prove their worth. Or join the mounting piles of bones in the desert.

British blood soaked these lands, and for what? She scowled. Oil fields and the Suez Canal, she'd been told. When she'd been on leave at her family's home in Cairo at Christmas, she'd questioned her father about the rationale behind the British push into Jerusalem. Despite his work at the Foreign Office, he failed to provide her with a satisfactory answer. The British had secured the Canal two years earlier, and she hadn't heard of oil in Jerusalem. The leadership in London had never dressed wounds or held soldiers' hands as they wept over lost limbs. Anger coursed through her.

As pink and yellow hues emerged on the horizon, the railroad tracks and road connecting the troops to the white canvas hospital tents shimmered like a river. She wished she could watch the sunrise. But today she had to answer for her temper and her weak attempt to see justice done.

To think she faced censure because she'd saved a life. The wrong life.

Just one week earlier she'd been ordered by a doctor to leave a soldier to die. *"We can't waste time on him when others are more likely to survive,"* the doctor had said. She'd disagreed and treated the soldier anyway. Now she faced a disciplinary hearing for it.

The rims of her eyes burned. Protocol didn't matter if she forgot her humanity. James wanted her to apologize. A wise, penitent response. But she was tired of pretending the rules always made sense.

"Ginger! On your way back already?" Beatrice ambled toward her, dressed in full uniform.

"I thought you were still sleeping." The sight of her friend set her nerves at ease.

"I heard you slip out. I thought I would come and offer moral support." Beatrice scanned Ginger's face. "Did you not sleep well?"

"I spent the night regurgitating excuses."

"You know you did nothing wrong. Who cares if you have to apologize?" Beatrice squeezed her hand.

A few feet away, a sunbird chirped at their approach and darted from pale-purple flowers dotting the brush. Sunlight caught its black feathers and gave them an iridescent shimmer as it took flight. An unexpected lightness filled Ginger as it soared among the sandy hills. "I suppose so."

"James thinks they won't take any further disciplinary action against you if you apologize. I overheard him discussing it with the matron last night."

Oh James. His inability to help himself was both endearing and irritating. "I rather wish he wouldn't."

Beatrice smiled. "I think it's sweet of him to intercede."

"Yes, but there are enough whispers implying I get away

with too much because of his influence. That he's the only reason I'm at the clearing station."

Beatrice lifted her skirt as they started the steep descent toward the railroad tracks. "You do have an advantage between your family and your fiancé. No use denying it. And aren't you here, partially, for him?"

Beatrice's frank honesty wasn't always the easiest to digest, though Ginger appreciated it. She sometimes sensed a hesitation in other nurses to treat her as a peer, despite their equal rank. She'd shared too much about her past with Beatrice to deny the truth, at any rate. And Beatrice still did her the favor of mailing back the unopened letters that arrived each week from the man Ginger's father had wanted her to marry instead of James.

A screech and hiss announced the first train of the day approaching the casualty clearing station. Ginger and Beatrice darted across the tracks. Safely on the other side, they slowed. The empty train cars crawled past them through billowing smoke, about to stop at the railhead. Acrid cinders burned their nostrils.

At the bottom of the next hill, a few crude huts stood beside an enormous stone well, surrounded by a copse of tall palms. Ginger had never understood how vital these wells were until her work in the desert. A soldier she'd treated in Port Said had told her horror stories of entire regiments going half mad with thirst, digging into the sand in their desperation, only to fall victim to the heat.

Fortunately, the British found working wells all over Belah. Despite the abundance, the army insisted upon heavily chlorinating it, ruining their tea. The huts, with their thatched palm-branch roofs, were crumbling structures of stone and mud. The army had little use for them and most of them stood empty.

A strange guttural noise came from one stone hut as they neared it. Ginger and Beatrice stopped, exchanging glances.

"Probably a private in his cups," Beatrice said, her voice dry.

"And if it's not?"

Beatrice tugged at her arm. "If it's not, we still need to hurry along."

Unconvinced, Ginger broke away toward the entrance of the bigger hut, an arch without a door. She stuck her head in, resting one hand on the shoulder strap of her kitbag. Her eyes settled on a man's booted foot.

"What on earth ...?"

The foot shifted, then she heard a moan.

Ginger stepped inside.

"What is it?" Beatrice asked.

Ginger's eyes adjusted to the dim light in the hut.

The man curled on the ground was breathing raggedly, and blood soaked his shredded shirtfront. The instinct to rush to his side faded when she saw his uniform.

A Turk.

Panic rose in her chest. His serious injuries didn't mean he couldn't attack her. Even the British soldiers did, occasionally, mad with pain. "It's ... an injured soldier."

She approached him, scanning the ground. She didn't see any weapons, but he might have one hidden beneath him. His hands trembled, pressed against his chest. He didn't seem to notice her. His eyes were closed. What was she thinking? He was the enemy. She should report him. She already faced a disciplinary hearing for taking matters into her own hands.

She recognized some wounds on his arms—the unmistakable gouges left by barbed wire. Mud and sand filled his wounds. A nasty scratch was painful, this appeared excruciating. The poor man.

"It's a Turk," Beatrice gasped behind her. "Ginger, get away from him."

Ginger flinched. It would be simple enough, turning him over to the military police and walking away. She had her hearing.

But this man might die any moment.

She sank to her knees beside him, her stomach in knots. Gnats and flies swarmed around him. In this heat, they didn't distinguish between live and dead flesh. If he wasn't cleaned, he'd have maggots under his skin within hours. She pulled away the tatters of his jacket. His arms were heavy and unco-operative. One blood-soaked pant leg revealed a bullet's entry and exit wounds.

Ginger pressed her fingers to his slow, faint pulse. His neck and forehead burned with fever, his skin was slick. His eyes remained closed. Spittle bubbled by his lips. She turned his arms over, where the wounds continued. One, deep and close to his brachial artery, appeared to have a makeshift tourniquet over it, but it needed replacing.

"What are you doing?" Beatrice's voice rose in pitch.

"For Pete's sake, he's not a threat. If we don't help him, he'll die." Precious minutes would determine if he lived. She'd treat him first, then turn him in. She had most of what she needed in her kitbag, but she lacked medicine. Ginger faced Beatrice. "Go to the triage station and get morphine. Quickly."

Beatrice looked horrified. "What about your hearing?"

"His life is at stake, for goodness' sake." She removed cloth strips from her kitbag and met Beatrice's wide blue eyes. "Hurry, please."

Beatrice nodded and whirled around and left. Ginger wrapped a new tourniquet over his arm with the fabric strips. Carefully, she discarded the blood-soaked one. Her hands were sticky with blood by the time she finished.

She elevated his arm over his head and stood, wiping her hands on her apron. The man's eyelids fluttered, his limbs shaking. He was a tall, broad man, easily over six feet.

A satchel lay beside his body. If he had any identifying papers, they'd be in there. A few personal items were inside —a cigarette case, a lighter, and … a Bible? Most Turkish soldiers were Muslim. Further inspection revealed a stamp from the YMCA in Cairo. And the text was in English.

She stared at the Bible.

It made no sense.

His eyes opened, dark irises darting through the slits. He found her gaze and grabbed her by the forearm. "Help me," he rasped. "Help me, please, Sister."

Her jaw dropped. His English was perfect. And he'd even used the British term 'sister' rather than 'nurse.'

The incongruity furthered her unease. She scooted away. "Who are you?"

"Ah … Ahmed." His tongue seemed to stick to the roof of his mouth. "I'm known as Ahmed Bayrak. You must help me."

"I don't understand. Are you British?"

He shook his head. "An ally."

"But your uniform—"

"A d-disguise to spy on the Ottomans. They discovered me." He moistened his lips.

Could it be true? If he was an ally, it was her duty to help him, not just a wish. A knot in her shoulders unwound.

She offered him her canteen. Water poured from his mouth as he drank. "Only a little. If you've been without, it will make you ill." She pulled the canteen back.

"Help me. I have important information for my c-contact."

She wanted to believe him. But it wasn't up to her to discover the truth to his words, much as she wanted it to be so. "I'll treat your wounds." She chose her words carefully.

"And give you over to the military police. They'll be able to help you better than I."

He grasped her wrist. "No, you must not."

She stared at his hand, her pulse accelerating. What was taking Beatrice so long?

"Forgive me." He dropped his hand. "You cannot. The enemy h-hunts me. He will find me here."

She dug into her kitbag for the whistle, just in case. "There are no Turks here. You're in a British clearing station in Belah." Her fingertips collided with the cool metal, and her fist closed around it.

His eyes widened. "There's a spy in British intelligence. A traitor. He hunts me." He retrieved a bottle from his pocket with a shaking hand. "Take this. Bury it. Bury it. Please."

She hesitated and released the whistle. She took the bottle and rolled it in her palm. The glass was amber and lightweight. What was in it of such importance? "You want me to bury this now?"

"P-please. I beg you. It must stay safe. It's for Cairo Intelligence."

She wasn't about to dig into the hard, compacted dirt floor with her bare hands. In the corner of the hut a loose stone at the joint of the ground and the wall caught her eye. She pulled it out and tucked the bottle behind it.

She straightened as voices drew closer. Beatrice poked her head through the entrance. "I brought James."

Oh no.

James hunkered down past the entrance. He adjusted his glasses.

Ginger's shoulders hunched with embarrassment. *"I'll instruct Sister Thornton to fetch me if you ever get the idea to do something like this again,"* James had threatened when the news of her censure reached him last time.

"James, I—"

James crossed his arms. "I was waiting in the Mess for you. What are you doing? This is absolute madness."

Ahmed spoke again. "Thevshi. I must find Lieutenant Thevshi."

Beatrice and James both appeared surprised. Ginger hurried to Ahmed. "Where can I find him? Is he here?"

Ahmed shook his head. "No—he's with Cairo Intelligence. Send a wire. He'll come."

His words gave her an odd sense of hope. "Can Lieutenant Thevshi confirm your identity?"

James approached, his gaze fixed on Ahmed. "What's this about?"

Ahmed's shoulders heaved with exhaustion.

"He says he's a British ally, not a Turk," Ginger said.

Despite his obvious exasperation, James's tone was gentle. "The brass will sort him, dearest."

"But he says he'll be exposed to a traitor in British intelligence if we turn him over."

"But of course." James appeared unconvinced.

Ahmed's trembling increased, lines of pain etched on his features. "Did you at least bring the morphine?" Ginger asked Beatrice.

Beatrice cocked an eyebrow. "I did. I'm not useless." She held it out, along with a syringe.

Ginger sat and prepared the medicine. "He's gravely wounded, but he might survive with treatment."

James adjusted his collar. "What about your hearing? You'll be late. And this won't do you any favors. I won't have you sacrificing yourself for this man."

Ginger pinched the flesh of Ahmed's uninjured bicep between her fingers and injected him. "I won't ask permission to treat him. Report me if you like."

"I didn't say I'd report you." A flush came to James's pale cheeks. "I'm not going to."

She'd counted on that. "Good." She put the syringe down and reached for antiseptic. "Are you going to help me or not?"

Ahmed's labored breathing intensified. "You must believe me." His words came slurred. "The O-ottomans are ..."—another rasped breath—"... shell the railhead. — know their plans ..."

James pulled Ginger away. "Come with me." He tilted his head toward Beatrice. "You too."

They exited into the sunshine. Ginger faced them.

"What if he's telling the truth?"

James put a gentle hand on her shoulder. "And what if he's taking advantage of your kindness?"

Beatrice stepped beside Ginger. "He speaks English awfully well for a Turk."

Ginger gave her a thankful glance. Beatrice was too practical not to be fair. "If he's telling the truth, turning him over might get him killed. He's given us a way to verify his identity. Can't we at least treat him until we've found out?"

Beatrice appealed to James. "What if we put him in isolation? He won't be able to leave from there easily. And you could assign Ginger or me to attend to him in the meantime, to limit his contact with anyone else."

"He won't be able to leave. He's too injured." Ginger squeezed James's hand. "It isn't a terrible plan. Please."

James hesitated, then sighed. "Only if you go to your hearing. Now. Beatrice and I will see to his care. If you're late, it will increase your chances of a harsh punishment."

Beatrice nodded encouragingly. "We can do it."

Despite her reluctance, Ginger stepped back. "Start with his right arm. It needs immediate stitching. There's a wound on his torso that also needs debridement. And a gunshot through the left thigh."

James's eyes hinted amusement. "I am a surgeon, you know."

"Oh, and we should take his personal effects into safe-keeping. They're beside him."

"I will. My quarters aren't subject to inspection from the matron like yours are. Now go." James smiled. "Get on with it and make your apologies, Lady Virginia."

Ginger threw her arms around his neck. "I told you never to call me that." She kissed his cheek. "Thank you both. Wish me luck." She hurried toward the main path. The encounter with Ahmed had rattled her confidence about the hearing. An apology would be a bald-faced lie. She wanted to face the surgeon who'd reported her and give him a piece of her mind instead.

The matron of nurses, Miss Walsh, approached the well. "Sister Whitman. I've been searching everywhere for you. The commanding officer is waiting for you."

Ginger stumbled. The matron hadn't seen her leave the hut, had she? Heat crept up her neck. "Ah—yes. I came for the morning burials. Why don't you walk with me?"

The matron hesitated.

What if she had seen? She would never put up with them helping the soldier. At last, the matron fell into step beside her, and Ginger's shoulders relaxed.

They had just reached the officers' quarters, when a faint boom traveled from the Turkish stronghold at Gaza. A whistling sound cut the air followed by a fantastic crash nearby. Ginger grabbed the matron and dove off the path. Another deafening boom shook the earth.

Ginger covered her head with her arms. She rolled over and checked on the matron. "Are you hurt?"

The matron shook her head. "No ... no."

Ginger helped the older woman up. She dusted herself off, her ears ringing.

A black plume of smoke rose a few hundred yards away. The sound came again—an echoing boom, the screeching cry of a shell hurtling through the air, then a thunderous crash.

A medic ran past them. "Run for cover, Sisters! They're shelling the railhead and within range of the hospital tents!"

The matron twisted her hands. "Don't they know we aren't soldiers here?"

Ahmed's warning.

A wave of nausea crested in her as a rumble began on the nearby plain, the stampede of camels, horses, and men trying to escape each intermittent shell.

The wounded in the hospital tents needed immediate evacuation. Ginger ran toward the tents closest to the railhead.

Behind the row of tents, the train raced away, its whistle shrieking.

The matron caught her by the arm. "Sister Whitman, you will get yourself killed!" She pulled her back. "We must find shelter, immediately. Back toward headquarters!"

"But the men—" She wouldn't abandon them.

"Leave the soldiers to it. It won't do anyone any good if you're dead."

A high-pitched wail neared, like the strident cry of a thousand cicadas in the heat of a summer night. Yet it was empty, lifeless. A moment later, a shell tore through a hospital tent. A scream caught in her throat, shock rippling through her limbs as the cries of wounded men filled the air.

ACKNOWLEDGMENTS

If I've learned one thing is that it takes a village to write a book!

I wouldn't have been able to bring this project to completion without the help of some amazing people. They include:

C.S. Lakin, who I consider a friend in addition to being an incredible editor. Her suggestions lead to this prequel and I'm so glad for her continued guidance and help.

Robin Seville, whose keen editorial eye and knowledge of British English is invaluable to me. While I never would have guessed that a tarmac is for cars instead of airplanes like it is here, the help he offers me is immeasurable and wonderful.

My proofreader, Amanda Coleman. Thank you for helping me make this book have the spit-and-polish it deserves!

The Red Pen Crew, my beta readers, and Lisa Boyle who were all able to read this thing before it was ready and give me honest, constructive, and helpful feedback.

Patrick, my husband and investor. I promise someday we'll watch tv together again.

ABOUT THE AUTHOR

Annabelle McCormack writes to bring under-explored periods of history to life. She is a graduate of the Johns Hopkins University's M.A. in Writing Program. She lives in Maryland with her hilarious husband, where she serves as a snack bitch for her (lucky-they're-cute) five children.

Visit her at www.annabellemccormack.com or http://instagram.com/annabellemccormack to follow her daily adventures.

Manufactured by Amazon.ca
Bolton, ON